The Sister Switch

The Sister Switch

Jane B. Mason & Sarah Hines Stephens

SCHOLASTIC INC.

New York Toronto London Auckland Sydney
Mexico City New Delhi Hong Kong Buenos Aires

ISBN-13: 978-0-545-07802-3
ISBN-10: 0-545-07802-4

Copyright © 2008 by Jane B. Mason
and Sarah Hines Stephens

12 11 10 9 8 7 6 5 4 3 2 1   9 10 11 12 13/0

Printed in the U.S.A.   40
First printing, January 2009

To Geminis Everywhere

CHAPTER ONE
♪ CAITLIN ♪

Thwack! My sister's foot connects with the ball. It's headed right toward me, but I don't even bother to look up from my book. First of all, I'm right at a really good part. Second, despite the fact that I'm sitting in a chair placed in the middle of the goal in our backyard, I am one hundred percent positive that the ball won't hit me. It never hits me — Andie's kicks are too good.

"Score," Andie shouts as the ball sails into the high right corner of the net. "That's fifty-two!"

"Yeah, but who's counting?" I tease. Now that I've finished the chapter I look up for a second, and Andie flashes me a smile.

"I am, of course." She grins and raises an eyebrow.

1

I know she wishes I would actually play goalie instead of just sitting here reading, but that's never going to happen. I almost never play soccer with Andie. Besides, this book is great. I really want to finish it before school starts, which means I only have until . . . tomorrow!

I dive into the next chapter while Andie flops down on her back in the grass with her ball. Her head is on the ground to my left and I can feel her gazing up at me with her green eyes — eyes that are exactly like mine. Actually, her whole face is exactly like mine, with maybe a few more freckles from all of the time in the sun on the playing field. The only other difference in our appearances is that she *always* wears her shoulder-length thick brown hair pulled back, and I *always* wear mine down. Other than that, we're identical, as in identical twins.

"Hey, Cait," Andie says, and waits.

"Hey, Andie," I say back, giving up on reading and closing my book around my finger to mark my place. I take a look at her face and know exactly what's on her mind. "You're thinking about school, huh?" I can read her thoughts as easily as my novel. It's a twin thing. And I might as well give up on reading for now, anyway, because between my sister giving me the silent "let's talk" look and

2

my own excitement about starting school, I've read that last paragraph about five times. I'm still not sure exactly what it says.

Andie nods and tosses the soccer ball into the air over her stomach, catching it easily. "Can you believe that in less than twenty-four hours another glorious summer will be gone like the wind?"

I wrinkle my eyebrows and look down at her. Andie never uses similes like "gone like the wind." "Since when are you a poet?" I want to know.

"Didn't I tell you? I'm turning over a new leaf for junior high. I'm going to become . . ." she puts on her best serious expression and says, "scholarly."

I let out a whoop and shove her with my foot. "That'll be the day!" I laugh as I slide out of my chair and onto the grass next to her. "The same day I become a jock!"

It's pretty amazing, actually, how Andie and I can *look* exactly the same but *be* totally different. Andie is super-sporty and has an entire squad of friends. Mom says she has an "overdeveloped social life," and in the past it hasn't left her a lot of time for academics.

Me? I'm more into music than sports, and I love school. I always make honor roll and Andie keeps predicting that I will be the class valedictorian someday. I tell her it will never happen because I'd have to give a speech at graduation, which I would never do. Talking in front of a crowd makes my knees wobble and my stomach head for the hills. But maybe I'll be able to figure something out before then. After all, graduation is pretty far away.

One thing Andie and I do have in common, besides our looks, is that we are both totally excited about starting at Woodland. Being in junior high means we've conquered elementary school and are moving onward and upward — new teachers, new students, new everything!

"The soccer team at Woodland is awesome!" Andie announces, tossing her ball a little higher. "Did you know that last year they made it all the way to —"

"State, I know — you've told me a hundred times, remember?" In the fall Andie talks soccer nonstop, and if I didn't know how much she loves it, it might drive me a little crazy. Okay, a lot crazy. I try to act interested most of the time, but Andie knows I couldn't care less about anything that involves kicking, throwing, or running. I'm pretty sure that between the two of us, I didn't get a single sporty gene — Andie got every last one.

Which is fine by me, because I just want to play clarinet in the school band, and even more than that, in Jazz Ensemble. That's another great thing about junior high. Woodland has this crazy good jazz group that you have to audition for and everything. It may not be a state-ranked soccer team, but it's a really big deal to me. Apparently, not many seventh graders get in, but I've been working on my audition piece all summer while Andie was kicking soccer balls around with her friends. I am determined to make the musical cut!

Andie rests the ball on her belly and grabs my wrist to look at my watch — something else that's different about us. I wear my favorite turquoise watch every day, and Andie doesn't even own an alarm clock. As a result, she's always looking at mine.

"Only twenty hours to go," she announces. "In twenty hours Andie and Caitlin Kline will be bona fide junior highers." She jumps to her feet and starts bouncing the soccer ball off her head, a skill she mastered when she was, like, six. I smirk as I watch the ball bounce off the tippy-top of her forehead over and over. My sister can't stay still when she gets excited. She can barely stay still when she sleeps!

"I just wish there could be more sports every day," she says with a sigh.

"If you were always playing sports, when

5

would you have time for math?" I tease, sitting up. Math and Andie have a kind of hate-hate relationship that goes way back. I brush the grass off my back and stand, pulling my chair out to the sideline.

Andie rolls her eyes at me and gets right back to heading the ball without missing a single bounce. *Thunk! Thunk! Thunk!* The familiar sound feels hypnotic and settles my mind while I think about tomorrow. I can't wait to walk through the doors and find my homeroom and see my best friend, Maddie.

Madeline Bright is something else. I met her at my first music recital when I was five, and we knew right away we'd be friends. She's funny and smart and an amazing flute player. She's also a spectacular talker. Maddie has been in Maine for more than a month, visiting her grandmother. And even though she calls me twice a week, it's not the same as being together.

Andie's team of friends, on the other hand, has been around for most of the summer. They all went to the same soccer day camp and have gotten together almost every day to try to bruise one another through their shin guards — something they apparently get a kick out of.

"Hey!" a voice calls out from the other side of the high wooden fence that surrounds our yard. I don't even have to look to know who it is — Olive Bruger, Andie's best friend. Andie and I have known Olive since preschool, when our mom still dressed us alike. She used to be best friends with both of us. In fact, the three of us used to spend so much time together that we joked that Olive was our long-lost triplet — even though, with her strawberry-blond hair, blue eyes, and gangly legs, she looks nothing like us.

A second later Olive's head appears just above the fence in the spot where the honeysuckle doesn't grow. She climbs over and Andie lets the ball hit the grass, then passes it to Olive. The black-and-white ball rolls to a stop in front of Olive's sneakered feet and she kicks it back, barely even looking. Without being asked she steps into the goal so Andie can start taking shots while I take a seat in the shade.

"Can you believe it's tomorrow?" Olive says as she blocks a shot. "Have you picked out your outfit yet?"

Andie shrugs and kicks the ball again, sending it flying into the net. "I dunno. Something clean, I guess. Probably jeans. Oh, and my new sneakers." That's typical Andie. She couldn't care less about clothes. I, on the other hand, have already laid out three different outfit options. Or should I say, I have narrowed my selection down to three.

"How about you?" Andie asks Olive as she sets up for another shot. "What are you gonna wear?"

"I was thinking of something a little dramatic," Olive replies with a wave of her hand. "Maybe that red hat my aunt Susan gave me. And maybe my Groucho glasses?" She's kidding about the glasses, but not the hat. Olive likes to be colorful, and she doesn't mind drawing attention to herself. In preschool, when Andie and I were wearing matching pastels, she'd show up in these crazy stripes and colorful polka dots. Sometimes she'd even come to school in her old Halloween costumes. As we got older, Olive was in all the plays, and usually got the leads, she was so good at it. Olive is all about drama and sports . . . in that order.

After blocking the ball and sending it back with a swift kick, Olive turns to me as if she's going to ask me what I'm planning to wear. I hope she will, because I'm dying to get a second opinion. But before she can speak the ball sails right by her — and into the net.

"Get your head in the game, Bruger!" Andie teases with a laugh. Olive pretends to scowl at the ball and then kicks it back out.

"That's it, Kline. No more easy goals for you."

I half wish they would ask me to play, just so I could join in the conversation. Sometimes I miss Olive. When the three of us were best friends we did everything together. Then last summer, the one between fifth and sixth grade, we all decided to go to sleepover camp. Our moms were about to sign us up when Andie came home with a flyer from Soccer Starz, a sleepover soccer camp. Needless to say, she was dying to go.

"But I don't like soccer," I'd said quietly. I pictured a whole summer of stumbling around the field, nursing skinned knees and jammed fingers . . . not to mention an ego bruised from being the last one picked, over and over. Soccer camp would turn my summer into one long gym class. *Not* my idea of fun.

Andie had looked totally guilty and quickly snatched the flyer from Mom's hand. "Right, of course," she'd said. "Forget it."

But I've known forever how much Andie loves soccer, and if she wanted to go then I wanted her to go, too. "No, you should go," I'd said. "It sounds really great."

9

"Maybe we could find you a music camp," Mom had suggested. That sounded pretty good, and we did. So while Andie went to soccer camp I went to music camp, which as it turned out was beyond amazing. We played all kinds of music, got to see live performances, and even played a concert in the park at the end! Maestro's Music Camp was where I learned how much fun it is to play in a band. It's so much better than doing recitals or solos. Playing with a group takes the pressure off. Since Maestro's, I am all about ensembles.

Olive and Andie had a great summer that year, too. They came back closer than ever and talked nonstop about all the stuff they'd learned at camp. They even had a few new sporty friends, including these two girls named Tara and Ivy, who are together so much I call them by a single name — TarandIvy.

I think it was that summer when Andie and I stopped doing every little thing together and started hanging out with different groups of friends. It wasn't like we stopped getting along. We still talked about stuff and sometimes we had even more to say since we'd been apart for chunks of time. Usually I think our differences make us closer — and those differences are probably a good thing. Don't we share enough already?

But there is one problem: I miss Olive.

I look down at the book in my hand, my finger still marking my place — only two chapters to go and a little less than twenty hours until junior high. I decide to finish up in my room and try on my outfits so I can make a final decision on what to wear. After that, I can practice my clarinet. My audition piece is almost ready, and so am I. Woodland Jazz Ensemble, here I come!

CHAPTER TWO
⚽ ANDIE ⚽

Ah, the first day of school. I am so ready for this! "Watch out, Woodland!" I say excitedly as I hop off the bus and glance over my shoulder at my sister. Caitlin is standing on the last step in new jeans and a green shirt that even I can see shows off her eyes. She looks great. But she's not moving. "Come on." I grab her hand and pull her off before all the kids waiting stampede and squash her flat.

"Don't pull so hard!" she says as I drag her through the crowd to the main doors. "I was trying to savor the moment!"

"Savor later. Let's get in there!" I tell her. Caitlin can be such a slowpoke. It took her half an hour just to get dressed this morning, and even longer to eat her cereal. I would have thought she'd be rushing out the door. My sister is crazy about learning.

And as we walk up the wide path toward the main two-story building I can't help but think that Woodland looks like a great place for it. Of course, I am most intrigued by the gymnasium wing off to our right. The large, low building is clearly different from the rest of the school and has a giant banner that reads: GO, WOODLAND WRANGLERS! I already know what it looks like inside since we came for the Open House over the summer. It has pullout wooden bleachers, a huge scoreboard, glass-back basketball hoops, and real locker rooms. Behind the gym, up on a flat rise, is the field, with big outdoor bleachers and a track ringing the grass. I have a feeling I'll be spending a lot of time there. But first I have to get through my classes.

Inside, the halls are crowded with students. Administrator types are scattered around, directing kids to their homerooms. I weave through the masses until I find a serious-looking woman with a clipboard and a messy bun.

"Andie and Caitlin Kline," I announce. I bounce on my toes, barely able to contain my excitement. I can't wait to get to homeroom and see who's there!

The woman gazes at us from behind a pair of half-glasses and smiles kindly. "My, don't you two look alike."

"Really?" I ask, feigning surprise and giving her a shocked face that would make drama mama Olive proud. "You think so?" I shoot Cait a sideways look. How many times have we heard that? Five million?

Caitlin tucks a lock of dark brown hair behind an ear and her face turns bright red. I am always embarrassing her — she thinks I take things too far. But life is for having fun, and it's not like I'm being rude or anything.

Bun Lady shoots me a look — I guess she doesn't appreciate my comment — and holds out two slips of paper. "These are your homeroom assignments," she explains. "You're in different rooms." She points to my homeroom just down the hall, and then to the stairs Caitlin will have to take to hers. "You'll get the rest of your schedule from your homeroom teachers."

"I wonder if we'll have any classes —"

"Room fourteen!" a voice interrupts by shouting in my right ear.

"Score!" a new voice shouts on my left. "We're all together!"

Tara and Ivy have appeared out of nowhere. They're flanking me like we're already on the field so they can read over my shoulders. Tara has just gotten her light brown hair cut in an ultra-short bob, which looks really good on her. Ivy's long blond locks are woven into a neat braid that hangs down between her shoulder blades. They're both dressed in shorts and T-shirts, their standard uniform.

"Welcome to Woodland!" Bun Lady says cheerfully. "Have a great first day!"

"Thanks," Caitlin tells her. We start down the hall and I pull ahead of Tara and Ivy so I can talk to my sister for a sec before we go our separate ways.

"Want me to walk you to your homeroom?" I ask, grabbing her wrist to check her watch. She holds her arm out patiently, even though I know she wishes I'd get my own watch instead of constantly checking hers. The thing is, I'm just not an accessory girl. I'm strictly jewelry free. I'm even letting the holes in my earlobes grow in.

I eye the two tiny hands on my sister's watch. Looks like we still have a few minutes before the first bell.

"No, thanks. I'll be fine," she says with one of

her "I can take care of myself" smiles. She gives me those sometimes when she thinks I'm acting like Mom. What can I say? I like to look out for my twin.

"This is a school, remember?" Cait reminds me.

"Point taken," I say sheepishly. "You're in your element." I'm about to give her hand a good-bye squeeze when Tara and Ivy both start pulling at my arms. I can feel myself being dragged away.

"There's Olive!" Tara and Ivy squeal in unison. They drop my arms and run over to say hello.

"See you la —" But before I can say good-bye a body pushes between me and my sister.

"Caitlin!" Maddie Bright rushes up, her blond curls bobbing wildly, and throws her arms around Caitlin. "Oooh, I missed you. Are you ready for Jazz Ensemble? I've been practicing like crazy. Your shirt is adorable, is it new? I'm in home-room two eleven. Where are you? I hope we're together. We just have to be." She stops talking long enough to glance at the slip of paper in Cait's hand. "Ooooooh, two eleven. Perfect, we *are* together!" She throws her arms around Caitlin again. If talking were a sport, Maddie would be a first-class athlete. I have no idea how she does it. Finally, she notices me standing there. "Hi, Andie!"

Maddie says, her blue eyes wide. "How was your summer?"

"It was great," I tell her.

"Me too. Maine was great. Lots of blueberries and lobster. I think I ate a hundred lobsters . . . not really, of course." She giggles. "But I could have! Lobster is so good!"

The five-minute bell rings, interrupting Maddie and signaling that it's time to get to class.

"Oooh, we have to go! Our homeroom is on the top floor!" Maddie squeals, pulling Caitlin away.

"Look for me at lunch — I'll be sitting with the cool kids," I call after them.

I smirk when Caitlin rolls her eyes. Then she gives me a little wave. "See you!" she calls as she disappears into the crowd.

"Ready?" Tara and Ivy ask. They've reappeared beside me and now they have Olive in tow.

I smile, because am I ever.

All my classes should be as hard as homeroom — attendance, announcements, and a few forms to fill out. My schedule is okay, too. After homeroom I have social studies — not too terrible — and then English, health, science, and lunch. After lunch I have math, but to make up for it I have gym immediately following. Top that off with Spanish and music appreciation and my day is done. Cake! 'Cept for the math part.

The trouble with math is that I got stuck with Mr. Mosely — the infamous Mr. Mosely, aka the Number Cruncher. Rumor has it he's the toughest math teacher in the school. And when I get to fifth period I discover math class is every bit as hard as I was afraid it would be. The good news is that I have math with Olive and we got seats together at the back of the room. But I'm in class for all of five minutes before I'm certain that my illustrious junior high career is taking a turn for the worse.

Okay, first I should explain. Contrary to popular belief, I don't hate math that much — not really. I just don't have the patience to sit still long enough to get through all the problems. I like to cut right to the chase. And right now I'm in the back row near the window, where the smell of the freshly mowed soccer field keeps drifting past my nose, and all I want to do is get out there and spend the rest of the day chasing a ball around.

From up here on the second floor I can actually see the field behind the gym. The soccer nets are all set up and ready to go — like me. Except the nets are enjoying the breeze and fresh air, and I am trapped in math for another forty minutes.

Suddenly, Olive jabs me in the ribs with her elbow, which, I have to say, is pretty sharp. I look up and notice that everyone else in class has their hand raised. Quickly, I raise mine, too, and flash Olive a smile. Olive is a total team player, or as she says when she's doing her drama stuff, an ensemble thespian. I can always count on her to save me from embarrassment . . . or at least to try to.

At the front of the room the Number Cruncher looks expectantly at yours truly from behind a pair of black square-rimmed glasses. "Andie Kline, can you answer the question?" he asks severely.

With a jolt I realize I don't even know what the question is, and since Mosely's gaze is as intense as a hawk's, there's no way I can get Olive to whisper it in my ear. My hero can't bail me out of this one.

I sit up straighter since there's no point in trying to back out. "Could you repeat the question, please?" I ask, trying to sound casual and self-assured. But Mosely is making me so nervous my palms are sweaty!

"Can you identify the mean, median, and mode of the number sequence on page twelve?" Mr. Mosely says evenly, but he's giving me a look that clearly says "pay attention the first time."

Ugh. Now I wish one of my classmates would throw up or something. Anything to get Mosely's steely gaze off of me. Because even though I hear him perfectly, I have no idea what the answer is. At all.

"You should remember this from sixth grade," Mosely says.

All around me hands are waving in the air, living proof that I am the last seventh grader on the planet who doesn't know the answer.

Mosely waits for exactly two seconds, then calls on a boy up front.

"Eight, seven, and five," he rattles off.

I groan inwardly and fight the urge to slide under my desk. One thing is for certain — I haven't scored any points with my new math teacher.

CHAPTER THREE
♪ CAITLIN ♪

"Isn't junior high the best?" Maddie bubbles as we head to the locker room after lunch for fifth period. It is time for the class I've been dreading all day.

I smile in spite of myself. One thing I love about Maddie is her great attitude. The girl can get excited about anything . . . even gym class. And I have to agree that, for the most part, junior high *is* the best.

So far I love my classes, especially math and English. They have a salad bar at lunch — with croutons. Yum! The band room is new and has amazing acoustics, and I can't wait for Jazz Ensemble auditions next week. So even though now it's time for the humiliation and torture teachers call physical education, I try to count my blessings. One good thing is the fact that Maddie is in my class. There's nothing better than a little moral support in desperate times like these.

I look over at Maddie's smiling face. "Yup, pretty great . . . so far," I agree, trying to look upbeat.

Maddie gives me a worried look and opens her locker, which is next to mine. Then she grabs me by the shoulders. "Repeat after me," she instructs quietly. "Gym rocks."

I roll my eyes. "I can't say that," I tell her. "I'd be lying."

Maddie giggles. "Yeah. You're right. But it might not be so bad. . . ." She trails off as she pulls her clean gym shirt on.

I hang my clothes in my locker and put on my own unflattering gym gear, marveling at the fact that this stuff is what Andie *likes* to wear. Then, before I can think too much about how to get out of this class, Maddie grabs my arm and pulls me out the door.

"Can you believe how nice Mr. Kolb is?" Maddie asks, changing the subject back to music and our new band teacher. "Soooooo nice. And the auditorium has a real stage with lights and everything."

I'm not sure if she's trying to distract me or if she's just being Maddie, but either way I'm grateful. "You're going to look great playing your flute up there," I tell her as we follow the rest of our class outside. Apparently, when the weather is nice, gym classes meet on the main playing field. Tarandlvy are right in front of us, but they're so busy talking soccer strategy that they don't even look our way. Behind us, Tina and Carla, two girls I know from last year, are giggling over a couple of boys I've never seen before. I'm about to roll my eyes at Maddie over this when I see Coach Tangara and swallow hard instead. Whoa.

"All right, line up in alphabetical order!" she bellows. Coach Tangara makes an impression. She's stocky, has short, graying hair that sticks out from under her baseball cap, and is wearing tube socks pulled up to her knees. She sounds like she's talking through a bullhorn, but she's not. I try not to wince as I head to the middle of the line with the rest of the K's, L's, M's, and N's.

"Anderson, Kailee," Coach Tangara blurts, reading from her clipboard.

"Here," says a soft voice at the end of the line.

"Louder!" Tangara shouts.

"Here!" Kailee repeats.

"I can't hear you!"

"HHEEEERRRE!"

23

I look at Maddie as a feeling of panic washes over me. Coach Tangara seems like a cross between a drill sergeant and a Roman gladiator.

"They call her the Tank," Jesse King, the boy standing next to me, whispers. I gulp as my turn comes closer. I can see why.

"Kline, Caitlin."

"Here!" I try to shout, but when I take a big breath to do it I inhale some saliva and end up coughing like crazy. I turn red, hacking loudly. When I finally catch my breath I gasp, "Here!" Even when all I have to utter is a single syllable, talking in a group is just about impossible for me. It's mortifying.

The Tank gives me a look but doesn't say anything. Thank goodness.

When roll call is over she blows her whistle. "All right, three laps around the track. Meet back here. Go!"

Everyone takes off running, but I just stand there like a deer caught in headlights. Laps? That's almost as bad as public speaking! This is just another way for me to humiliate myself. When it comes to putting one foot in front of the other with any sort of speed I am doomed to trip. Repeatedly. I'm pretty sure attempting to run three laps in a row might warrant a call to 911.

"Something wrong?" Coach Tangara asks, raising an eyebrow at me and bunching her lips together.

"Uh, no, not exactly, but . . ." I'm stuttering like a fool when Maddie jogs back and grabs me by the arm for the second time in ten minutes.

"Come on, Caitlin," she encourages as we jog away. "It's just jogging."

Before I can stop myself I shoot Maddie a nasty look. She knows about my issues with coordination.

"Sorry," she adds, obviously feeling bad. "But the sooner we start the sooner we'll be done."

Easy for her to say. But I follow her and start jogging at the back of the pack. Hopefully, back here fewer people will witness my shame.

Things start off okay and by the end of the first lap I feel a flicker of hope. Maybe I can get through this without any major injuries. On the second lap I trip once but manage to recover. It's not pretty, me flailing around like an out-of-whack windmill, but I come through it unscathed. When I finish the third lap, my mouth is hanging open in shock. By some miracle I am still on my feet! I'm coming to a stop when it happens. My right shoelace has come loose and I pin it with my other foot. When I try to lift my right foot, it won't budge and down I go.

Somebody says "Timber" softly, but not so softly that I don't hear it, and I can feel my face turn fire-engine red as I lie sprawled out on the grass.

"Back in formation!" Coach Tangara bellows over the giggles of my classmates. While the others scramble into place I sort of crawl over and manage to stand and inspect the damage. I don't seem to be bleeding, unless you count my ego, which is hemorrhaging profusely.

"On Wednesday we'll be having our physical fitness assessment," Tangara announces. "It's a new requirement mandated by the state to help combat the obesity epidemic our country is currently facing."

Still trying to catch my breath, I look down. I may be a klutz, but I'm not obese. Does *everyone* have to take the assessment? Unfortunately, I don't get a chance to ask.

"The assessment will consist of three categories: endurance, strength, and agility. Each category will be scored. Students must earn an average score of seven out of ten in order to pass the assessment." She shoots me a look right when she mentions passing. Guess she noticed I wasn't tearing up the track during laps. "Anyone who does not pass will be required to enroll in the Healthily

26

Ever After after-school program, which begins next week," she finishes.

I feel my stomach lurch. "I am in perfectly fine shape," I want to shout. "I just do terribly in athletic situations." Andie says I overthink when it comes to using my body; I say I'm a menace to myself and others. I have taken more nosedives than any girl my age. So — an athletic *test*? I will choke for sure. I will be the biggest loser out there.

But it's not the humiliation that worries me — it's Jazz Ensemble. It meets three days a week . . . *after* school. I can't do some after-school fitness program! I've been waiting to do Jazz Ensemble for years! I am not giving up Jazz Ensemble to practice chin-ups. But I can feel the panic rising. I am never going to score a seven in those categories.

My life in junior high is officially over, and it's barely even started.

CHAPTER FOUR
⚽ ANDIE ⚽

Mr. Mosely is still giving me the evil eye when the bell rings. There's no question about it — even without a watch I'm certain that my first Woodland math class was the longest of my life, hands down.

"Talk about a drill sergeant," I whisper to Olive as we finally head to gym.

"Oh, I don't know," she says as she slings her backpack over her shoulder. "The Number Cruncher didn't seem that bad to me — definitely not as bad as the stories. And at least we got to review. My math skills went into hibernation over the summer. It's nice of him to wake us up gently."

Gently? Is she kidding? Mr. Mosely-the-math-menace has a gaze of steel. I don't know what his

28

median is, but his mode is all mean. Still, there's no use harping on it. I decide to shake off my math class like I shake off a bad soccer play — you just have to move on. And I've got something to look forward to . . . something that starts in exactly four and a half minutes! I can feel the smile spreading across my face but then I spot Cait coming out of the gym. She looks all pale and shaky, like she's seen a ghost. My smile fades.

"Are you okay?" I ask, even though I know we don't really have time to talk. But Caitlin looks awful, which makes me *feel* awful.

Cait shakes her head and wipes a tear on her sleeve. She's obviously struggling to pull it together.

I put a hand on her arm. "Whatever it is, we'll figure it out," I whisper. Cait hates drawing attention to herself so I know she won't want to get into it now — whatever *it* is.

She looks back at me, her green eyes glistening and full of doubt. Then she pulls away and heads off down the hall.

With a lump in my stomach, I push the door to the locker room open. When we were little, Cait and I would always cry when the other twin did — even if we were responsible for inflicting the tears in the first place. And even though I

29

am not tearing up, I still feel like that on the inside. When she hurts, I hurt.

"What's up?" Olive asks as she pulls open her gym locker. She's studying my face and she looks worried.

"Something's going on with Cait," I reply, slipping on my favorite soccer shorts. "I don't know what it is, but it doesn't look good." Tears on the first day of school are not a positive sign.

Once we're changed we head out to the field. Finally, I get to hit all that freshly mowed, ready-for-play grass. We gather at the edge of the track with Mr. Dakin, the new assistant football coach, and wait for him to take attendance.

"All right, have a seat if you like, but stay close. I've got a lot of names to call out and I want to get through them fast so we can move on to the good stuff."

Olive and I exchange smiles and collapse on the sod.

"Aster, John." Mr. Dakin begins, calling the names one by one. When attendance is out of the way it's time for some laps. "Three times around," the coach instructs, "and the person who beats me gets to sit out the laps next class!" He drops his clipboard and takes off around the track with everyone racing after him. Olive and I finish with the front of the pack and drop onto the grass, out of breath. We're fast, but *nobody* manages to beat Mr. Dakin.

"Nice job," he tells us as the last few runners straggle in. "Looks like everyone here will do all right on the assessment on Wednesday." Then he rambles on about the obesity epidemic in the United States and how the state is trying to combat it with exercise programs in the schools. "The assessment will test your strength, endurance, and agility, and the results will be averaged. Anyone who doesn't score a seven out of ten will have to take a required athletics class after school."

No problemo, I think. Soccer uses all three of those things, and a lot more. Sounds like the assessment will be a piece of cake, and fun, too. Even the fitness class sounds kinda cool.

"And now for some real fun," Mr. Dakin says with a smile. "Follow me." He leads us over to the far side of the field where someone has set up a little obstacle course. "I've set this up so that you can try your hand at the types of strength, endurance, and flexibility activities that will be on the test," he explains.

I eye the course. It looks like a standard boot-camp-type drill with a rope wall, tires to run

31

through, a bar for chin-ups, and a place to measure flexibility based on how far you can reach forward while sitting with straight legs.

"Line up and we'll all run through it a couple of times," he tells us. Olive and I are the first ones up and we breeze through, one behind the other, then we sit back to watch the rest of the kids.

"Go, Sandra!" Olive encourages a girl we know from elementary school. I know I should cheer, too, but my sister's sad face keeps popping into my head. Even though she didn't give me any clues, it looks like her first day of junior high has turned into a disaster!

When the bell rings I rush into the locker room to change. I try to find Cait in the halls before seventh period and again before eighth, but can't. Finally, the day is over and I race to my locker. I bang it open and grab my messenger bag, then dash to the curb where the bus is already waiting. As soon as I'm inside I spot my sister in the back, slumped on one of the seats next to Maddie.

Maddie is talking as usual, but she shoots me a desperate look and moves over to make room for me. She even lets me interrupt, another sign that things are not okay.

"Caitlin," I say, reaching for her hand, "what's the matter?"

Cait looks up at me, her face all red and blotchy. "Gym!" she whispers hoarsely. "Gym is the matter! How can anyone stand that stupid class? No offense," she adds, shooting me a dejected look. "I know you love sports, but physical education is ruining my life!"

"Is this about the assessment?" I ask quietly.

Caitlin nods, her eyes filling with tears. Maddie and I both shift in our seats so that nobody can really see her. She doesn't need the humiliation of being known as a crybaby on top of feeling miserable. Especially on the first day of school.

"It'll be fine," I assure her. "All you need is a little practice. I can help."

Cait shoots me a look. "Between now and Wednesday you can rewire my brain so it communicates with my feet? I don't think so." I hate to admit it, but she's got a point. Because even though Caitlin could be a great athlete if she wanted to, a miraculous two-day transformation is pretty unlikely.

"Maybe the fitness class will be cool. It sounds kind of fun," I say, trying to look on the bright side.

Cait's face says it all. Fun and fitness are not on the same page in her book. And then it dawns on me, she has other plans for after school.

Jazz Ensemble. I get it now. And I know that nothing I say is going to make Cait feel any better. So I just sit there next to her for the rest of the ride home, wishing I had a magic wand I could wave over my sister that would give her just a little bit of my athletic skill — just for a day, or even an hour.

Things aren't looking any better when Caitlin shows up at the breakfast table the next day wearing jeans and a T-shirt. And nothing else. No bracelets, no earrings . . . not even her watch! (Um, how am I supposed to know what time it is?)

"Shouldn't you be dressed for school?" Mom asks Caitlin, glancing at her as she opens the refrigerator. She pauses long enough to raise a single eyebrow. She knows as well as I do that Cait lays out her outfits and accessories before she goes to bed and is always ready on time. Caitlin's outfit today is totally un-Caitlin. She only dresses down on chore days, and would never consider going to school *un*accessorized.

"I *am* dressed for school," Caitlin says. She dumps some cereal into a bowl and takes a bite without adding milk. The dry, crunching sound is totally depressing, but not as depressing as seeing my sister wearing an outfit that could be mine.

On the bus Cait stares quietly out the window, and I hardly see her at school all day. By the time dinner rolls around I can tell things are dire. Cait just sits there pushing her peas around her plate, not eating or saying anything. On a normal night we would be chatting and answering questions from our parents — probably rolling our eyes at most of what they said. But not tonight. Only two days into junior high and Cait's a total wreck.

It doesn't take Dad long to pick up on Cait's gloom. "Are you all set for your Jazz Ensemble auditions, Cait?" he asks, trying to cheer her up. "I heard you playing when I was doing laundry Sunday. Sounded great." He grins before adding, "I know I'm biased. But I think you're a shoo-in."

Cait stops chewing the one bite she's managed to lift to her mouth. I try to shoot Dad a look, to let him know he's picked the *wrong* topic, but he doesn't see me, and my leg doesn't reach far enough for me to kick him. Cait drops her fork onto her plate, looking like she might cry.

"Honey, what is it?" Mom asks, her eyes filling with concern. She looks from Cait to me. If my twin can't talk I am prepared to do it for her — something Mom counts on. But Cait has been holding back long enough.

"I can't do Jazz Ensemble!" she cries. "I'm going to have to live Healthily Ever After instead!"

My parents exchange a "what is going on?" look over the platter of salmon in the center of our round kitchen table, then peer at Cait, waiting for her to say more. Neither of them says a word — they know better than to put Cait on the spot. But Mom starts twirling a lock of hair behind her right ear, something she does when she's stressed. And Dad has that wide-eyed, panicked look he gets. The silence is killing me. My leg is bouncing a mile a minute under the table. They might be able to wait, but I can't.

"They're giving everyone a fitness assessment in gym, and kids who don't score well will have to take an extra fitness class after school," I blurt.

Cait's eyes glisten. Mom twirls faster. Dad puts down his fork, still looking confused. "You're in perfectly good shape, Caitlin," he says gently. "You'll do fine."

I agree with the first part of what he says, but I'm not so sure about the second. She *could* do fine . . . if only she believed it was possible. I'm just not sure all that certainty about her uncertainty can be undone before fifth period tomorrow.

"Don't worry about it so much, honey." Mom stands up and rubs Cait's shoulders. Easy for her to say, I think as I look at Cait suffering away.

I rack my brain for a way to help Cait out of her mess. It doesn't seem fair that she won't even get a shot at Jazz Ensemble, the thing she's been looking forward to all summer. I keep going over the problem in my mind as I clear the table, help with the dishes, and do my homework. And then, while I'm brushing my teeth, it hits me. I beam at myself — foam and all — in the mirror. Because I know *exactly* how to solve Cait's problem.

CHAPTER FIVE
♪ CaiTLiN ♪

Andie and I are standing in front of the bathroom mirror brushing our teeth. I feel like the end of the world is coming when all of a sudden Andie stops brushing and starts freaking out. She's gesturing like crazy, waving one arm in the air and trying to talk with her mouth full of toothpaste.

"Spit!" I tell her, stepping back a little in case she loses it and sends foamy slime flying. It's times like these I'm thankful we have one of those long bathroom counters with two sinks.

My sister leans over and spits into her sink, then does a quick rinse. "I've got it!" she cries, still a little frothy around the mouth.

"You've got what, rabies?" I ask. My mood is not good. And to tell the truth, I'm not counting on it getting any better until a year from now, when I'll have the chance to realize my dream of getting into Jazz Ensemble. But I shouldn't take it out on my sister.

"No, I've got a solution for your problem," Andie insists, grinning and wiping away her foam.

"Really?" I ask, even though I'm ninety-nine point nine percent positive that there *is* no solution for my problem.

Andie gives me one of her "I'm the greatest sister you could ever hope for" smirks and spreads her arms wide. "Yup, and you're looking at it," she says.

It takes me less than five seconds to figure out what she's going to say. She doesn't even have to explain . . . but of course she does, anyway.

"I can be you for gym tomorrow."

"You can take the assessment for me?" A little spark of Jazz Ensemble hope warms a tiny spot inside me. But then, as I think about it, my heart drops back down to my toes. "We'll get caught. Remember last time? And we promised we wouldn't do that anymore."

Andie rolls her eyes. "Do you want to do Jazz Ensemble or not?" she asks pointedly.

"More than anything," I answer.

"That's what's important here, Caitlin," Andie insists. "Forget last time. That was a party prank. This is serious."

"But everyone was so mad." I cringe at the memory of Olive's birthday party of several years ago.

We traded identities for fun, and everyone was completely fooled . . . until Mom showed up. She blew our little joke the second she walked in, right before Olive's surprise karaoke debut. The revelation totally stole Olive's thunder. It was all anyone could talk about for days — except Olive, who dished out a week of the silent treatment. When she finally started talking to us she made us swear we would *never* fool her like that again. A few of the other kids didn't think it was very cool to be fooled, either. And Mom, who didn't buy it for a second, made us swear we wouldn't try to put anything over on any adults for stuff that mattered — like dental appointments or exams.

"But this isn't stuff that matters," Andie reasons. "I mean, it's just a little fitness assessment. Of course it matters to you that you pass, but we know you're fit. You just have uncooperative feet. And it's not like it's actually school or anything. If it were, *you'd* be helping *me*."

Well, I have to admit, that's true. My heart gives a flip when I realize we might actually be able to pull this off. "Maybe it'll be okay. Just this once," I say, a little hesitantly. And Andie fans my spark of hope into a flame.

"Are you kidding? It'll be great!" Andie grabs a hacky sack off the bathroom counter and starts knocking it off her head, knees, and feet, like she's juggling without arms. She's doing that moving thing again, and her excitement is catching. I feel fidgety myself.

"But, wait," I tell her as I ponder this idea a little more. "You can't just ace the test — nobody would believe it. You have to do just well enough to pass. And you have to *act* like me, not just look like me, or everyone will know." The last time we switched all we had to do was eat cake like each other.

"No problem," Andie grins, kicking the sack onto the counter next to the sink. She pulls the rubber band out of her hair, releasing her ever-present ponytail. Shaking her hair into her eyes, she dons a thoughtful expression. Then she picks up the toothpaste tube and pretends to blow into it like it's my clarinet, humming off-key.

"Uncle!" I complain, holding my ears. But I'm smiling, too.

41

"Now you do me!" Andie says, putting the toothpaste back on the counter and grinning.

Without hesitating I pull my hair back into a ponytail, plaster on a grin, and start waving to invisible schoolmates. "Hey, did you catch the game?" I call out, walking in place down an imaginary school hall. "Man, that was intense. Triple overtime. Yeah!" I pretend to slap five with someone. Then I grab the sack off the counter and whack it with my foot. Only instead of going straight into the air and coming back for another tap it sails into the hall. I chase after it, almost body slamming Dad, who is coming down the hall with a basket stacked high with folded laundry.

"Look out, A. You almost fouled me," he jokes, calling me by Andie's nickname.

"Sorry, Dad." Grinning, I duck back into the bathroom before he gets a good look.

Andie is grinning right back at me, and I don't have to say a word because we are both thinking the same thing: If we can fool Dad we can fool the school crowd (okay, so his vision was blocked by clean underwear, but still).

"Fifth period tomorrow?" I ask.

Andie nods. "That means you get to go to my math class!" she crows.

"Andie Kline, do you have an ulterior motive?"

I put my hands on my hips and give her a good scowl.

"No!" she insists, but she can't hide her smirk. "It's just a fringe benefit. Mosely is seriously tough and impossible to please."

"Okay, but I am not doing your homework," I tell her.

"Fine." She pretend-mopes for a millisecond, then perks up. "This'll be fun. Meet me in the second-floor bathroom at the end of lunch. And don't wear a skirt," she adds. "I don't do skirts, not even to the locker room and back."

As if I didn't already know. "Fine with me, but you can't wear sweats, or one of your fifteen soccer uniforms," I shoot back. "Make sure you match. And we can't tell *anyone*!"

"Agreed." Andie nods. "I promised Olive we wouldn't try to pull any fast ones, and we don't want to upset her again," she says gravely.

I nod, too. "And Maddie would be hurt if she thought she was being left out of a secret."

"So it's just between us." Andie offers her hand, and we shake on it and head to our rooms, grinning.

Our plan is so clever, so simple. And it solves all of my problems. What could possibly go wrong?

CHAPTER SIX

⚽ ANDiE ⚽

From the second I wake up the next morning all I can think about is fifth period . . . and the swap. At breakfast Caitlin and I keep giving each other the eye and giggling in between bites of cereal. She's wearing a simple tank top and more-stylish-than-I-would-wear jeans. I'm wearing what I always do — regular jeans and a T-shirt.

"Well, I'm glad someone's feeling better this morning," Mom says as she fills our orange juice glasses. She's clearly spotted Caitlin's smile and dangling earrings. "I'm sure everything will work out all right with that test, Caitlin." She smiles encouragingly.

"What? Oh yes," Caitlin mumbles, turning a little red. "I think everything will be just fine." She shoots me a look, then wolfs down the rest of her bowl of

O's, takes her dish to the sink, and dashes to the bathroom to brush her teeth. Keeping secrets is not one of Cait's strong points, but I follow her to the bathroom to remind her that even though Mom is tough to fool, she's not a mind reader.

"Sorry. I guess I'm just nervous," Cait admits. "Aren't you?"

"Nah. I'm excited. No math." Smiling, I pull her toward the front door. The sooner we get out of the house the better, because one sideways look from Mom, and Cait might just confess everything.

"What's the hurry?" Mom says. She's sitting down at the table with her coffee and the paper. Normally, we would let her read us our horoscope (we're Geminis). But today is not normal.

"Don't want to miss the bus," I say over my shoulder as Cait grabs her backpack.

"Cait, you forgot your orange juice!" Mom calls as I push my sister out the door. "Hey, is everything okay?"

"Fine, Mom. But I just brushed my teeth." She makes the "blech" face. "You can have it!" she calls back.

When the door clicks shut behind us, Cait breathes an audible sigh of relief. "Do you think she knows?" Her face is flushed and her voice is all fluttery.

45

"Of course not," I assure her. "But I'm glad we got out of the house before you spilled the beans!"

As we climb onto the bus I feel excited and nervous at the same time. I'm dying to talk out all the details one more time, but Cait grabs a seat next to Maddie a few rows back. I take a seat alone and drum my fingers on it. Probably just as well, I tell myself. Thinking about the switch is nerve-racking enough. Talking about it might just put me over the edge!

At school, I see that Olive is already at our lockers and she runs up to me as I make my way down the hall.

"You won't believe it!" she cries. "The school play is *Grease*!" She is clutching my arm and practically jumping up and down, so I guess doing *Grease* is a good thing. Then she grabs her water bottle and starts singing into it. "Tell me more, tell me more, like does he have a car," she belts out. She's even adding a little choreography as she does it.

"That's great," I tell her, but I'm not really paying attention. Maybe she's so fired up about the play she won't notice how out of it I am. "What part are you going out for?"

Olive drops the water bottle into her book bag and her face turns suddenly serious. "I can't decide," she admits. "The lead is always tempting, but Rizzo is so much more interesting. . . ." She trails off, a dreamy look in her eyes. I'm pretty sure she's imagining opening night, or maybe a Tony acceptance speech.

I see my sister walking down the hall, catch her eye, and get the jitters all over again — it feels like we're planning a surprise party or something. I drum my fingers on my locker until Olive reaches a hand up and makes me stop. How am I ever going to make it to fifth period without exploding?

During social studies, the one class Caitlin and I share, I sit near the front and stare straight ahead. Every time I look at Caitlin my heart starts to pound like crazy and I have to look away.

"Are you and Caitlin in a fight?" Olive whispers to me from the across the aisle.

"No!" I fire back after making sure the teacher's back is turned. Mr. Hansen, the social studies teacher, is kind of strict. "Why?"

Olive shrugs. "It just seems like you're ignoring her or something."

I force a little laugh, hoping it doesn't *sound* forced. Olive doesn't miss anything! Mr. Hansen gives the two of us a stern look and I bury my head in my notebook.

A couple of minutes later, Olive whispers hoarsely, "Stop moving."

"Huh?"

"Stop moving your foot. You're jiggling it like mad."

I look under my desk, and sure enough, my leg looks like it's a cell phone on vibrate. I put my hand on my knee to make it stop.

"What's up?" Olive is looking at me like I've gone a little cuckoo. "You're acting like it's game day or something."

"Nothing is up," I say, tossing my ponytail and trying to keep my leg still. It's a lot harder than it sounds. Olive is making me nervous. She already thinks something's going on, and we haven't even done anything yet! I keep remembering how icy her cold shoulder is. I nearly died of frostbite the week she stopped talking to me.

Later in class while we're doing a work sheet, I glance behind me and see Maddie whispering to Cait. I can't see my sister's expression because her face is hidden behind a curtain of hair. Is she as antsy as I am? I feel like I've been at school for days, and it's only first period. I try to focus on the teacher, who's telling us something about the U.S. census — but it's not exactly the most scintillating topic. Especially when all you can think about is your supersecret plan to rescue your sister's musical career.

I'm not sure how I survived the endless morning hours, but finally it's lunchtime and, after picking apart my sandwich and ditching Olive, Tara, and Ivy, I'm racing to make it to the second-floor bathroom before the five-minute bell. Crossing my fingers and hoping that nobody else is in there, I push open the door. Right away I spot a single set of shoes under a stall door — Caitlin's. Whew! Even though she has nine thousand different pairs, I'd know my sister's shoes anywhere.

"Ready or not," I call, a little louder than I mean to. My voice sounds funny. I am so excited!

"Here we come," she answers as she slips off her shoes.

I duck into the stall next to hers so we can toss our clothes back and forth. I slide my sneakers under the stall and she passes me her flats. We trade tops and then jeans.

Before you know it we're standing in front of the mirror getting down to the finishing touches.

"I can't believe I have to change *again* for gym in less than two minutes," I say excitedly as I look at our reflections.

"Sorry." Cait looks apologetic for exactly half a second, then gets back to business. "Remember, my locker is number twelve. Take your hair down," she tells me. I pull my ponytail holder out and hand it over.

"Wipe off the lip gloss," I instruct, passing her a paper towel. She hands me her backpack. "What do you have in here, the whole library?" I groan. She might be clumsy, but my sister has to have some serious muscle power to lug this thing around all day.

"You did your math homework, right?" Cait wants to know. I roll my eyes. I might not be a star student, but I'm not a total slacker, either. "Of course. It's in my book."

She pulls out a crumpled piece of binder paper and holds it up. I give her a nod. "Yup, that's it."

Caitlin examines it at arm's length like it smells. "Uh, okay . . ." she says, sounding unsure.

We turn and look at ourselves — and each other — in the mirror. My heart is pounding. Cait looks at her watch — wait a second, she still has her watch on. And her earrings.

"Give me that," I say, snatching the watch off her wrist and glancing at the time. "And the earrings, too." I force the wires through my half-closed holes. Ouch! The bell is about to sound.

We check ourselves in the mirror one last time.

Our eyes meet, and we smile at each other's reflection. Then we burst out laughing.

"Ready?" I ask.

Caitlin nods. "Ready." She opens the door and we step into the hall.

"See you here right after, okay?" I say. It's going to be tight to change back for sixth period.

"Okay, Cait," Caitlin replies as I head off down the hall. I hold back another nervous chuckle and try to imitate my sister's walk, which is not quite as fast as mine since she's always worried about tripping over her own feet. By the time I get to the stairs I'm starting to feel like I *am* Caitlin. I let my hair fall forward around my face and hoist her bag o' books higher on my shoulder.

Just then Gena Griff, one of Cait's band buddies, flags me down from the other side of the hall. "Hey, Caitlin," she says, a little breathless. "Do you have an extra reed?"

"Read?" I ask, a little confused. Is this some new term for a book recommendation? "You mean, like —" I stop myself as it dawns on me. "Oh, a reed . . . for your clarinet." I am about to slap my forehead but realize that is not exactly a Cait move. So I push my hair back behind my ear instead.

Gena gives me a funny look. "Uh, yeah," she says.

I shake my head and my hair flops everywhere. "Sorry, I don't," I say, though I have no idea if Caitlin has any extra reeds or not.

Looking a little disappointed, Gena moves away just as the real test approaches. Tara and Ivy are walking right toward me, arguing about who is the better soccer player, Beckham or Ronaldinho. I walk a tiny bit slower and wait to see if they'll ask me to weigh in. (It's Beckham, of course.) But when they look up they give a quick wave, and keep right on bickering. They don't recognize me at all!

Feeling totally exhilarated, I drop Caitlin's stuff in her locker, throw on her gym shirt, shorts, and shoes, and hurry out to the field.

Coach Tangara is waiting, looking totally official in her referee uniform. Mr. Dakin is here, too. They're both wearing stopwatches and carrying clipboards.

"Line up!" Tangara bellows as everyone falls into place. I hurry over to the line, wondering if it is best to stand next to Maddie or avoid her. Before I can decide, the boy next to me gives me a weird, kind of fearful, look.

"You want the Tank to give you extra laps or something? We line up alphabetically!" he hisses.

"Right!" I say, moving to the middle of the line.

My Maddie issue is solved, at least for now. I lean out to give her a smile and a wave.

"Where have you been?" she mouths.

I mime hurrying and shrug as Tangara starts taking attendance. "Anderson, Kailee," she bellows. I start at the noise and almost jump back. She is *serious*, and the class knows it.

Everyone shouts "here" so loudly you'd think we were in the army. But attendance only takes a few minutes, and then the fun part — the part I'm here for — begins.

"M through Z, you're with Mr. Dakin. He'll break you into groups and time each test. A through L, you're with me."

I've got no problem with that, of course. Andie — I mean Caitlin — Kline is ready for whatever the Tank can throw at her.

First we have to run a lap, which is a quarter mile. I try to take it at an easy, Cait-like pace, but it feels so great to run — especially when I remember where I'd be if I weren't helping my sister — that I cross the finish line way ahead of Maddie and a lot of other kids.

"Did your mom put coffee in your cereal this morning?" Maddie asks, bending over and trying to catch her breath once she finishes. "I've never seen you run like that. And what happened to you at lunch? I was waiting for you in the cafeteria for, like, ever. You barely ate and then you just left your tray."

I try to look exhausted as I take a sip from my water bottle. "Sorry. I needed to get focused," I say, laughing just a little. "Andie coached me last night." I smile, hoping that's enough of an explanation. Maddie is still looking skeptical when we're interrupted.

"Caitlin, move on to the rope wall," Tangara instructs. "You too, Madeline."

"Here we go." Maddie sighs, stepping up.

"Just take it easy," I whisper to myself as I watch Maddie struggling with the wall. It's a lot taller than the one we climbed on Monday, and Maddie's feet keep getting tangled in the rope. I can hear her talking to it like it's the rope's fault.

"Get off of me! Lousy rope. Let go. You're holding me back."

I have to bite my tongue to keep from cheering and shouting pointers, or even just telling Maddie to be quiet and focus on the climb. Caitlin would never do that. But finally she finishes.

"Thank you," she says to the rope, dusting off her hands and blowing a curl out of her face.

"You're up, Caitlin," Tangara calls. Only, for a

second, I forget that I'm supposed to be Caitlin, and I just stand there like an idiot. "Caitlin!" she shouts again. "Caitlin Kline!"

Whoops! I realize my mistake just as Maddie comes over and gives me a little shove toward the rope wall. "Come on, Caitlin. You can do it," she assures me. It turns out my bad move was actually good because it made me look hesitant — very Cait!

"I can do it," I repeat, to sound like I'm trying to talk myself into it. Just remember to do it kind of s-l-o-w-l-y, I think in my head.

I start out struggling on purpose, but then I just start thinking about getting to the top and my plan to take it slow goes right out the window.

Maddie is staring at me like I have green hair when I get back to the line of kids waiting their turn. I think it's the first time I have seen her speechless.

"Way to go, Caitlin," someone says from the sidelines.

"Right," Maddie says, finding her voice and looking at me askance. "Way to go."

"Andie's pointers were really good," I fib. "I think they might be helping." I twist Caitlin's earring nervously. My holes were practically closed and the earrings feel tight and itchy.

"I think they're *definitely* helping," Maddie agrees. "Maybe she can give me some pointers, too."

Gladly, I think. But I can't help but wonder if she's suspicious.

The tire run for agility goes better than the first two tests — I mean worse, because I manage to remember all the way through that I'm Caitlin, not Andie, and even fall once or twice. But Maddie is still looking at me funny, and since I'm a little afraid of being grilled about my odd behavior I leave her lounging on the bleachers when I'm finished, making a big show of having an empty water bottle. I head for the drinking fountain at the other end of the field.

On my way I slow down when I see a strangely familiar floppy-haired boy playing soccer with a group of guys. Then I stop dead in my tracks. I stare at the familiar face, desperately trying to place it — and the person it's attached to — when someone does it for me.

"Over here, Scooter!" Mike Duff calls as the blond floppy-haired boy passes him the ball.

I flinch at the name and do a double take. Like Mike said, the guy is Scooter — Scooter Vanderhoff. Cait and I went to preschool with him and he used to drive me crazy. Really crazy. But in a totally different way.

First off, his name is Scooter. Unless his parents hate him, that was a lousy choice of names. Who calls their kid Scooter? Second, when we were four he followed me around the park every day throwing sand at me. And third, he always used to wear pants that just never seemed long enough. They always ended a couple inches above his socks.

But as I watch Scooter play soccer, I realize that things have definitely changed. Scooter is too busy dominating the field to throw sand at anyone—he's become a seriously decent soccer player during the last eight years. He's also a lot taller than he used to be. He doesn't have any finger paint on his clothes, and even though he's wearing shorts, they seem to be a normal length. And, maybe most important, his bank shot is incredible!

I squeeze my eyes shut. What in the world am I thinking? With my eyes still closed, I turn back toward the fountain. My stomach is all fizzy. Is this how other girls feel about boys? Does Scooter count as a boy? Am I getting the flu? I lean over for a drink and can't resist another peek.

Looking under my own arm I catch a glimpse of blond locks and then totally blast myself in the face with water by accident.

Spluttering, choking, and blinded, I can hear Maddie laughing from the bleachers. I turn toward the sound, wipe my face on my sleeve, and give a pageant wave. At least *that* move was Cait-ish, right?

Then suddenly I see the black-and-white ball heading my way, fast. Without thinking I turn and kick it back onto the field to the open position — a perfect pass. And a perfect setup for Scooter to score a goal. He kicks it in and his team cheers. A few of the guys cry foul.

"Okay, fine, we won't count the goal," Scooter shouts to the whiners. His smile is playful. "*If* you let her play on our team." He looks at me out of the corner of his eye to see if I like the idea, and all thoughts of acting like a klutz fly right out of my head. I can't hear myself think over the pounding of my heart. Or maybe I'm just not thinking. The guys agree, and I jog onto the field before I can remind myself that Caitlin despises soccer.

Back on the bleachers Maddie sits up straight and looks like she is about to call the school nurse.

Oh, well. It's too late now, I think. The damage

is done. I chase the ball down and use some of my best moves. I know I am showing off, but I can't help it. I can feel a certain pair of eyes following me and I don't want them to stop.

Scooter doesn't say much, so I am pretty sure he doesn't remember me from day care. But when he compliments my free kick my stomach does a double backflip. And I thought my pre-switch jitters were bad!

When the Tank ends class I head toward the locker room to look for the portion of my brain that has not turned to mush. I try not to pay too much attention to the direction Scooter is going and marvel at the difference a few years can make. . . .

"Caitlin Kline!" Tangara calls. This time I remember who I'm supposed to be, halt, and head back to where she's standing. I try not to look nervous. Did she notice that I didn't seem to know my own name earlier?

"I was watching you on the soccer field," Coach says. I gulp. "You're good. I hope you'll be going out for the team."

Relief washes over me. "Of course —" I start to say. Then I remember . . . I'm *still* Caitlin! "I mean, um, I have some other after-school obligations," I mumble apologetically.

"You're kidding, right?" Suddenly, Scooter is right next to me and my brain is once again MIA. "You *have* to go out for the team!" His smile is warm and a little lopsided. "You're really good." He compliments me — I mean Caitlin — sincerely, and I feel like it would be a slap in the face to say no. Scooter and the coach both want me to do this, and I hate to let people down.

"Well, I can probably work it out," I say, looking from the coach to Scooter and back. "When are tryouts?" I ask innocently. The date is emblazoned in my head, but right now my head is on vacation.

"Next Tuesday, after school," Coach rattles off.

"I can run drills with you at lunch tomorrow . . . if you want," Scooter offers. Is he a little nervous, or does he always look at his feet when he talks?

"I'll be there!" I tell both of them.

"Great!" Coach Tangara pats me hard on the back and walks off.

Holy cow. What is wrong with me? Coach and Scooter still think I'm Caitlin, who does *not* play soccer. Ever. And how in the world am *I* supposed to go out for the team if *I* am busy being Caitlin?

My mind reeling, I head to the locker room. Only one thing is certain. It looks like I'll be Caitlin once again tomorrow at precisely eleven-forty A.M.

CHAPTER SEVEN
♪ CAITLIN ♪

I wiggle my toes in Andie's sneakers and watch my sister speed toward the gym. Though my heart is hammering in my chest a million beats a minute, I know that I am saved . . . and that she is my hero. It's so great to have a sister who will do anything for me. Right then and there in the hallway I make myself a little promise to do something great for Andie, too (like maybe tossing out these stinky sneaks . . . ew). Her sportiness is truly admirable. And her outgoing personality is the best. If the girl had an ounce of style sense she'd be downright dangerous! But before I can think of a way to implant fashion clues in her brain I am surrounded.

"Practice after school?"

"Dribbling drills?"

Tara and Ivy have me on both sides. They stare at me with expectant eyes until I break into a sweat. Think like Andie, I tell myself. "Uh, sure," I stammer. So *not* Andie. They're still staring. "Where?" I ask, trying to sound more confident and hoping that this is the next logical question.

"The field?" Tara says. The "duh" is clear in her voice. "Where were *you* thinking, the cafeteria?"

I roll my eyes and force a laugh. "Haven't you guys ever heard of a joke?" TarandIvy laugh. I might have actually pulled that one off. "See you there." I hold my hand up for a high five. But when neither of them slap it I just wave. It's a pathetic attempt at a save. Then I hurry toward the relative safety of math class.

Andie's class meets in the same room I have advanced math in, so it's easy enough to find and look like I know where I'm going. I stroll in with my shoulders back and start to slide into my desk Andie-style — head thrown back, knees everywhere, craning my head to look around and say hello to everyone.

"Excuse me?" Randall Suarez is suddenly standing next to my seat and giving me a funny look.

"Hey." I wave. I didn't know he and Andie were pals, but it shouldn't surprise me. She talks to everyone.

Randall keeps standing and staring in a not-so-friendly way. It takes me a second to realize what the problem is — I am sitting in *my* seat, where *I* sit for advanced math. Apparently, this is Randall's seat this period and now I realize I have no idea where Andie sits!

Luckily, I spot Olive sitting next to an empty seat, one of only a few. That has to be Andie's spot. I mumble my apologies and make my way over, grateful that Olive didn't see me acting so completely Cait-like.

"Where've you been?" she asks casually as I sit down.

"Bathroom," I tell her. And I'm glad it's the truth. I am a terrible liar.

While Mr. Mosely takes attendance I smooth out Andie's homework. It looks like she slept on it . . . while having some serious nightmares. It also appears she guessed at most of the problems because she hasn't written out any of the steps, but her answers aren't half bad. If she had just taken the time to show the steps she could have aced the whole assignment. As it is, she probably got about eighty percent right. Pretty amazing, since I'm ninety-nine percent positive she did it in about fifteen minutes.

It's obvious that Andie could be really good

at math if she would just slow down and take a second to think about what she's doing. She might even see that math can be fun — like a game.

"Are you okay?" Olive whispers. She leans over my desk to see what I am doing. I have erased all of the random marks on Andie's paper and fixed a couple of her answers. Suspect behavior in Olive's eyes, no doubt.

"Great. Never better." I grin and hold up my hand for a five. Olive doesn't slap it any more than TarandIvy, so I quickly make a peace sign and a mental note: trying to high-five Andie's friends only makes you look stupid — and, more important, *not* like Andie. I wish I could hide my reddening face behind my hair, but it is pulled back so tight there's no place to take cover.

I slouch down in my chair and try to look relaxed, aloof, Andie-ish. It's not easy. Olive has gotten up and is standing by my desk looking at me . . . waiting for something. I feel like the game is up, but the period only just started. I rack my brain, straining to come up with what Andie would say in this situation. She would be calm. She would wait for Olive to speak. "So . . ." I prompt.

"So, can I have your homework?" Olive asks, holding out her hand.

Of course! She's collecting work for Mr. Mosely! I push my paper across the desk. "Well, since you asked," I joke. Olive smiles and snatches the paper out of my hand. I may not be great at this, but if I could just relax, like Andie would, I'd do better.

Thankfully, I *am* great at math. As soon as the homework is collected, Mosely starts writing out some equations on the board. I watch closely as he makes perfect chalk figures. It's mesmerizing. How can Andie not think Mr. Mosely is great?

I copy the problems and hope that my twin is doing okay with the Tank. But just thinking about Coach Tangara ties my stomach in knots, so I refocus on math.

Mr. Mosely calls for our attention so he can go over a few things.

"Can anyone tell me how to convert a fraction into a decimal?" That's an easy question, and before I can stop myself my hand shoots up.

"Andie?" The baffled look on his face makes it clear I am *not* acting like Andie. But I don't want to make matters worse, so I answer quickly and slump farther down in my seat.

"Nice to see you paying attention." Mr. Mosely nods and gives me a smile before turning back to the board.

Then I silently congratulate myself. I can't help it! They say compliments from Mr. Mosely are pretty rare, and I, I mean Andie, just earned one!

"Did he just smile at you?" Olive whispers. "That's the first time I've seen his teeth. Good to know they're clean and straight." She kicks me lightly under my desk and I give her a thumbs-up, silently praying that that's a normal Andie move.

But Olive is looking at me like I just sprouted a horn between my eyes. "What's up with you today?" she asks.

I shrug. "Cait helped me last night." Then I lean over the desk to start on the assignment before she can say anything else. Olive keeps staring and I feel *totally* exposed without my hair down. I keep reaching up to tuck it behind my ear only to find it is already pulled back. Relax. Think *Andie*, I coach myself.

Finally, Olive turns her attention to her assignment and starts humming one of the songs from *Grease* really softly.

The class works silently while Mr. Mosely grades the homework at the front of the room. Since I said I wouldn't do Andie's homework for her, I just get the problems set up. It's hard not to write out the answers, though. I just love the crossover-butterfly shape multiplying fractions makes. It's like math art.

There are still five minutes of class left (and I am trying to look like I'm doing the problems without actually doing them) when Mr. Mosely interrupts us to make an announcement. "Class, I would like to invite you all to be a part of the Mosely Mathletic Squad. The squad will compete against other Woodland squads once a month, either during lunch or after school. An abbreviated competition will take place tomorrow at twelve fifteen. Not only is it fun, but you will earn extra credit for participating . . . which, judging by your homework today, some of you will definitely need."

Ooh! Mathletics. I remember hearing all about Mathletics during a special assembly at our old school about all the stuff that goes on in junior high. It's where I learned about Jazz Ensemble, too. At the time I thought Mathletics sounded cool — kind of like a live game show. But it was all wrong for me, because it would mean speaking in front of a crowd. My tongue goes numb if more than three people are looking at me at once. And I get super-queasy. Andie, on the other hand, loves competition . . . and she can talk to, or in front of, *anyone* without feeling the slightest bit sick.

67

My mind is spinning as I gather Andie's stuff and head to the door. Mr. Mosely is standing by the exit.

"Nice job on your homework, Andie."

Another compliment! I grin widely, then tone it down to a small smile. "Thanks."

Olive shoots me a look, and Mr. Mosely asks us to stay a moment.

"I thought maybe you two might be interested in going out for the Mathletic squad." Mr. Mosely taps on his clipboard with his pen before holding the sign-up sheet out to us.

I freeze and my heart pounds. I'm so tempted I actually start to reach for it. Then Olive grabs it first. "Yeah, come on, Andie. Let's do it! It'll be just like playing sports." She elbows me and writes her name.

Andie does thrive on competition, I remind myself. "Count me in," I tell Mr. Mosely as Olive passes me the board. I sign Andie up, grinning. Then I realize something. There's one teensy-weensy part of Mathletics that isn't up Andie's alley: the math part.

As we walk out of the room Olive is smiling with half her mouth. "I had no idea you liked math." She sighs. "I never really wanted to tell you before, but I think fractions are kinda fun," she says sheepishly when we are out in the hall.

"Me too!" I agree.

"I like the crossover when you times them," Olive confesses. Her eyebrows go up in this funny way I had almost forgotten about that makes her look like a kid who is in trouble, but too cute to punish. And right then, as I look at those eyebrows, I realize how much I have been missing Olive Bruger.

You know, it's weird. Back when all three of us — me, Andie, and Olive — were *all* best friends, I always felt like Olive really got the few things about me that Andie didn't. Understanding the beauty in math, for example. It feels kind of like old times, except Olive isn't getting *me* now, she's getting Andie. So it doesn't really count. Then, suddenly, more than anything, *I* want to play on the Mathletic squad myself. Even if I have to do it as Andie. It's a perfect opportunity to take a chance, break out of my shell, *and* hang out with Olive.

I am all distracted when I suddenly remember I have to change. I glance at my bare wrist, mumble something about having to pee, and race for the bathrooms. I burst through the door to find Andie already there. "We have to switch again tomorrow," we say in unison.

CHAPTER EIGHT

⚽ ANDie ⚽

I walk into Caitlin's room without knocking (twin privilege) and flop down on her bed, belly up. "Take my temperature," I order her. "Please."

Cait, who up until this moment had been practicing her clarinet to some big-band music coming from her iPod speakers, lowers her instrument and looks at me like I am bonkers. Which, by the way, I am.

"Are you sick?" Cait asks, her face registering concern. She pads over to me in her bunny slippers and leans in, hiding her face in her bathrobe sleeve. "You'd better not get me sick before try-outs!" she says in her muffled voice.

"Don't worry," I console her. "Something is definitely wrong with me . . . but I don't think it's contagious."

"So what is it?"

"Don't laugh," I say, looking up at her sheepishly. "But . . . I can't stop thinking about Scooter Vanderhoff."

"Sandchucker?" Cait cries. She looks alarmed. She kills the music, lays her clarinet down on the desk, and sits down next to me. "This sounds serious," she says.

I pull myself up to sit and wrap my arms around my knees. I squinch up my nose and then confess everything.

"I know it's nuts. I know I swore I would never be that girl who gets all stupid and jellylike over a guy. But I can't even help it. It's like he's taken over my brain. All I can think about is the way his hair flops down over his left eye when he's playing soccer and how easily I could brush it back — right after I steal the ball and make a goal for my team, of course."

Now it's Cait's turn to look sick.

"Okay, maybe that's a little extreme. But have you seen how tall he is now? Have you seen his bank shot?"

"You mean he's in my gym class?"

"Uh, yeah!" I answer. I can't believe she didn't even notice!

"Do his pants fit any better?" she asks drily.

"Or does he still look like he's waiting for a flood?"

I cringe a little. "Uh, yes, as far as I can tell he dresses like a normal person now," I confirm solemnly. Leave it to Cait to reserve judgment until she finds out if the guy has an acceptable wardrobe. What does it matter what he wears? Or how he wears it? I'm talking about being boy crazy, here. Me!

Even though Cait is making me feel a little lame for going gaga over a preschool dork, I have to admit I feel better after telling her. It hasn't even been a whole day since I became strangely possessed, but keeping anything from Cait feels weird — like talking or eating after you go to the dentist and you're all numb and drooly. It's not natural.

Cait bounces a little beside me on the bed, looking confused and trying to wrap her head around my new and alarming state of mind.

"But you don't even like boys," she says finally.

"I don't," I agree. "Um, except for one."

"Scooter Vanderhoff . . ." Cait repeats, clearly in shock.

I wish she'd stop saying his name. I mean, I know who he is — and how stupid it sounds.

"I don't get it. How can you like *him*?"

"I know." I shake my head again. Scooter Vanderhoff. Scooter with the perpetual pink Popsicle mustache. Scooter put-that-Tonka-down-before-you-hurt-someone Vanderhoff. "I guess when I'm you, I just do." I shrug.

Cait's eyes get even bigger. "Is that why you have to be me at lunch tomorrow?" she asks, putting it all together.

"Yeah. He'll be waiting for me on the field. And he's going to do drills with me ... uh, well, you actually."

"Sounds like fun." Cait rolls her eyes and I suddenly realize she hasn't told me why she needs to be *me* tomorrow. When she said she needed to switch again, too, I was so grateful I forgot to ask her why.

"So what am *I* doing at lunch tomorrow?" I finally ask, sitting up.

Cait looks at the floor. Her chestnut brown hair falls forward so I can't see her face and she mumbles something about a game.

"What?"

"You're competing ... as a Mathlete on the Mosely Mathletic squad," she says guiltily.

A huge laugh bursts from inside me. I fall back on Cait's bed again and hold my middle, cracking

73

up so bad I think I might fly into pieces. Pretty soon Cait is laughing, too.

Finally, I catch my breath. "I can't believe you have to be me to do *math*!" I say, sitting up and wiping my watering eyes.

"I don't have to be you to do math. I have to be you so I won't get nervous competing in front of other people . . . so we can win the game," Cait explains. She looks a little put out.

"Sorry," I say quickly. "I get it," I assure her, standing up. "And I have to agree I *am* a winner!" I raise my eyebrows and flex a muscle. Cait delivers a swift kick to my rear end (she really should consider soccer more seriously), and we both collapse onto the bed again in hysterics.

The next morning at school Olive is bouncier than a basketball. I am already a little jittery thinking about running drills with you-know-who, so Olive's constant rendition of the entire *Grease* soundtrack is making me nuts.

"What's up with you?" I ask as we head for homeroom.

"Oh, I just can't wait for lunch!" she says, making big eyes.

My eyes get bigger, too. How does Olive know about what's happening at lunch? Caitlin swore not to tell, and even though I'm glad I told my sister about Scooter, I'm definitely not ready for anyone else to know! "What?" I finally stammer.

Olive stops humming and gives me a look. "It's pizza day," she says. Like, duh.

"Right." I breathe a sigh of relief. My secret is safe. But now my stomach is all butterflies. For a second I wish I could tell Olive everything, but I can't blow it.

"And after we eat, we are going to wipe the cafeteria with those other Mathletes!" Olive narrows her eyes and rubs her hands together like she does before opening night or a big game. The girl has an admirable competitive streak. I hadn't realized she was doing the Mathletic thing, too.

By the time lunch rolls around the butterflies in my stomach have stopped fluttering and are starting to dive-bomb. I rush to the bathroom to meet Cait — we have to do the switch fast so nobody gets suspicious. Luckily, she is already waiting.

"Hair down," she reminds me. Then she starts to laugh. "Never in a million years did I think *I* would be playing soccer at lunch . . . for *fun*. People will think I've totally lost it."

"If they do, they'll think it's a twin thing since I'm now a Mathlete." I grimace.

"I guess you're right," Cait agrees. She looks great in my jeans, tank, and sweatshirt. I look . . . well, not exactly ready for the field in her shorts and blouse, but it will have to do. At least she brought her cleats.

With my hair blowing freely, I make my way past the gym and out to the field. Cait's cleats feel funny — they've hardly been worn. I'm not sure why Mom even bought them but maybe it's because she likes to try to make everything equal between us . . . and maybe secretly still wants to dress us alike.

Scooter is already on the field, bouncing the ball on his knees. He looks cute with his half-untucked jersey and messy hair. I wave, feeling my head go all foggy. What is it about this guy? He passes me the ball smoothly and we start playing. It's nice how we don't have to talk. We have a great rhythm, passing the ball back and forth up and down the field. A couple of times I catch myself looking at his floppy hair and have to consciously refocus on the game. But there's an ease I don't usually feel when I play. I'm not pushing myself to make every move count. Maybe it's because I'm distracted . . . or maybe it's because I'm Cait and not my soccer-star self.

Whatever it is, it scares me a little that I might

really turn into someone I don't know, so when we stop passing and face off against each other I keep my eyes on the ball and pull out all the stops — looking only at the ball. I make a good steal and hustle toward the goal. Just as I am about to slam the ball into the top right corner (my best move, besides my header), my hair flies into my face. I splutter, kick, and miss.

"Aaah!" I flop down on the grass and look up at the sky, panting.

Scooter's face appears above mine. "Maybe you should wear your hair back when you play," he suggests. "You'd look good like that." I feel my cheeks getting hot, part embarrassed and part I-don't-know-what, and jump back on my feet to recover the ball. I kick it to him, a fast pass, quick and accurate.

He traps it and slams it into the net while I jog toward midfield, thinking how much more relaxed I felt before when I wasn't trying to prove any-thing. I wonder if Cait feels like that all of the time. She only ever competes against herself.

"Hey, can you show me how you did that header in gym?" Scooter asks, jogging up behind me.

Happy to change the subject, I agree, and we do a few head drills, bouncing the ball back and forth off our foreheads like trained seals as we sidestep the length of the field. Headers are tricky and can hurt if you don't do them the right way. About halfway down the field, Scooter takes one too low on his face. He covers his eyes and nose with his hand.

"Ow!" His voice is muffled.

"Ha! I finally gotcha back for all of that sand you used to throw," I tease.

Now it's his turn to blush. "Aw, man. You still remember that?" he shakes his head, his hand still covering his face. "I was hoping you didn't know it was me."

"How could I forget? I think I still might have a scar from one of those trucks you hurled at me." I'm grinning, which I hope is a clear sign that I'm over it.

He pulls his hand from his face and smiles at me. "So, was that you? I thought it was your sister I used to chase."

His blue eyes twinkle and I can't look away. "Uh. Was that the bell?" I mumble. I'm locked in his gaze and feel like I'm hypnotized. I swear if he told me to cluck like a chicken I might. But even in my stupid haze I know enough to avoid Scooter's question. I have no idea how to answer it, anyway, because at this very fuzzy moment I am not sure if

I am me or my sister. I just know I am having a lot of fun.

Picking up the ball and tucking it under his arm, Scooter asks me another tricky question. "So, tryouts are Tuesday. Want to practice again on Monday after school?"

"Monday?" I echo. Then before I can stop myself I answer. "Sure!"

CHAPTER NINE
♪ caitlin ♪

As I sit behind the Integer team table at the front of the multipurpose room wearing a huge purple Mathlete T-shirt, I can't help but wonder if Andie and I should have been born just one person. Her boldness, my brains, her speed, my diligence . . . if we were a single package we'd be unbeatable.

I look at Olive, who is sitting next to me in an identical T-shirt. She gives me a thumbs-up. The Mosely Integers just answered three questions in a row correctly. The Hansen Remainders, in their teal tees, look a little gloomy about being trounced. Mr. Mosely looks like he is about to crack *another* smile . . . the third I have witnessed this year. If he keeps this up his reputation might be in trouble.

I take a deep breath and prepare to ring the buzzer that's been set up in the middle of our table. I feel calm, confident, and completely at ease even though there are about two dozen people sitting across from us like an audience. They're watching and cheering us on.

Being Andie is great! I can act fast and blurt out the answers as they come to me — no hesitating, no second-guessing. And no nausea. It is totally exhilarating to be able to say and do what I want when I want to. Not to mention that my team loves me.

Since I answered the last question correctly I get to pick the next category from a list written on the blackboard they wheeled in for the occasion. "I'll take percentages," I say calmly.

Sean Ghast, our student emcee, reads the question from a blue note card in his hand. "To turn a fraction into a percent you should . . . "

Easy. I buzz in before Sean can even read through the possible answers. "Divide the numerator by the denominator and move the decimal point two places to the right," I tell him. I can see the whole process in my head.

"Correct! Another point for The Integers!" Sean announces. Jamie Sanjay adds another tally mark to our score on the blackboard while my team claps me on the back.

When the game is over (7–2, Integers, thank you very much!), Olive and I walk down to the cafeteria to get a drink. That's the other great thing about being Andie — hanging out with Olive.

"That was amazing," Olive says, but she sounds kind of hesitant, and she is looking at me in a weird, sideways sort of way. "I still can't believe you wanted to do this. I mean, I didn't think you would ever go out for something so, um, academic."

"I think it's good to try new things sometimes," I say, smiling uncomfortably. "And Cait is always saying that math is fun."

"Yeah, but you never believe her," Olive replies with a laugh.

"Okay," I say, kind of sheepishly. "But I do like winning."

Olive grins. "Yeah, that sounds more like it. You know what it reminds me of? When you and me and Cait used to play all of those board games in your basement. Man, we were obsessed!"

For a second I can picture the board games spread out all over our rumpus room. We used to have board game Olympics, playing every game we owned for days on end. Olive and I always beat the pants off of Andie, which drove her crazy. She could have won, of course, but she was always fidgeting or practicing cartwheels between turns. She didn't like to sit still long enough to finish the game or develop any serious strategy. And she always gave up when it started to look like there was a chance she might not win.

We *really* started beating Andie when she got into playing sports instead, and then she just stopped playing with us. She likes fast action . . . and winning streaks, and she got more of both on the field than with us. For a little while Olive and I kept playing board games without her, but it wasn't as much fun with only two players. And after a while Andie needed a goalie and Olive volunteered. So our board game days came to an end.

"Remember the Monopoly marathon?" I can feel a smile spreading across my face just thinking about it.

"Do I!" Olive's smile is as wide as mine.

We played one game of Monopoly for almost a month. We were determined to get to the end of a game and actually have one person win *all* of the money. Olive and I were so evenly matched (she had Park Place and I had Boardwalk, the only set of properties on the board not owned by one person), the game just kept going on and on.

"How could I forget the battle for Boardwalk!" Olive says, cracking up. "Man, Caitlin really nickel-and-dimed me on that one."

"Caitlin, right," I say, reaching up to touch my Andie ponytail. I almost forgot that *Andie* split her money between Olive and me and stopped playing after just a few days. She'd said, "I think this is why they call them 'bored' games," and then left us downstairs alone. And Olive didn't realize that right now she was talking to *Caitlin*.

"Yeah." Olive sighs, her smile disappearing in an instant. "That was back when Caitlin still talked to me." She brushes her strawberry-blond hair back and chews on her lower lip, looking totally sad.

My stomach lurches. "But I, um, Cait *does* talk to you, doesn't she?"

Olive looks at me like I am crazy. Maybe she and Andie have discussed this before.

"Are you kidding? Cait *never* talks to me anymore. The second I show up she disappears into her room with her clarinet or a book."

I feel my stomach twist. Do I really? "That's just because she doesn't play soccer and you and And —" I start to explain, but at that moment the real Andie, looking just like me except for the soccer cleats and flushed cheeks, comes walking up to us.

84

"Hey," she grins. Scooter Vanderhoff is right behind her. "Did you see us on the soccer field?" "Caitlin" asks.

Olive raises her eyebrows at me. Talk about bad timing, since I just said that Caitlin doesn't play soccer! Wait! You don't understand, I want to shout at Olive. "She's Andie! *I'm* Caitlin!" But I can't, so I glare at Andie instead.

"I've gotta change for gym," Andie says, giving me a "let's go" look. "The bell's about to ring."

"I'll go with you," I say. "I think I left my math homework in my gym locker." I start to follow my sister for our dynamic duo presto change-o, but Olive calls me back. Maybe she didn't buy my excuse!

"Andie, before I forget, can you do me a favor?" she asks when "Cait" is out of earshot. "I need someone to run lines with me before the tryouts for *Grease* next week. Do you have time Monday after school?"

"Sure." It's so great hanging out with Olive that I agree without even thinking, and then turn back toward the gym. "See you in class."

Olive looks at me for a second. "Yeah, sure." She shrugs. "See you there."

As Olive heads for math I realize there are two things wrong with the plan I just agreed to. First, I

85

don't like acting. Due to my public-speaking pho-
bia, performing is my worst nightmare — even
reading lines is pretty torturous. And second, I
was planning to practice my Jazz Ensemble piece
after school every day until auditions, including
next Monday.

But I console myself with another thought. It
doesn't matter if *I* can't run lines, because Olive
wasn't actually asking *me*. She was asking Andie. I
just need to remember to tell my twin what *she*
agreed to.

CHAPTER TEN

⚽ ANDiE ⚽

It's a long haul from the locker room to math on the second floor, especially after doing soccer drills all lunch and changing your entire outfit at the speed of light. Cait was so busy gabbing with Olive that she barely got my clothes back to me in time. And let me tell you, standing in a bathroom stall dressed in nothing but your underwear for five minutes is a little unnerving. I was sure there was going to be a fire drill at any second.

But Cait did finally manage to get to the gym, and I did finally manage to get back into my clothes . . . mostly. As I jog to class my sneaker laces are flapping on the tile floor. At least my underwear is safely under wraps.

"What took you so long?" Olive hisses as I slide into the desk next to hers. Mosely pretends he doesn't notice my tardiness, which can only mean that his math squad . . . my math squad . . . won the first Mathletic event. I say a silent thank-you to my twin, then make my excuses.

"Ran into Tara and Ivy in the hall. Big Beckham debate," I whisper.

Olive is still staring. "Must have been some debate. Your sweatshirt is on inside out," she tells me, half rolling her eyes.

Oh no! "Whoops," I say as casually as I can, pulling it off and putting it back on the right way.

All during math, Mosely is super-nice to me. Before he even asks for the homework he announces The Integers' big win and calls out all the kids who played. I feel funny taking the credit when I didn't really compete, but there's nothing I can do. So I act like it's no big deal, and silently thank Cait a second time for scoring me some points with Number Cruncher. He's like a whole new guy. If I didn't know better I would swear he was almost smiling. The only downside is, he is *definitely* looking at me to be on the ball in class. Now that I'm a math star I have to actually *be* a math star.

"Ms. Kline? Can you tell me the next step?" he asks.

"Move the decimal two places to the right?"

Giving math answers is new to me, so I can't keep the question out of my voice.

"Exactly." Mosely adds the point to the board and turns back to the class. "Everyone got it?"

Amazingly, I think I actually do. And as I start in on my homework I decide to try it Cait's way. I go slow. I write out the problems, and you know? It's not that bad. This absolutely confirms that Cait is a genius. Not because *she's* good at math, but because she thought *I* could be good at math. And she was right.

I am especially grateful that the homework is a breeze because outside on the field Coach Tangara's class is running laps, and the sun glinting off of a certain blond head is distracting me. Then I see Cait, lagging way behind. She runs like Frankenstein's monster, and I make a mental note that next time I am Cait I have to tell Scooter how tired I felt after our lunch practice so he won't think I'm a freak.

Olive catches me looking. "Do you think Caitlin has a crush on Scooter?" she asks.

I'm glad she's looking out the window when she asks, because I nearly bite the eraser off my pencil at the thought. "Ugh. No!" I say, maybe too emphatically. "Don't you remember how he used to try to maim us with sand toys?"

"Just wondering." Olive shrugs. "I mean, I can't remember the last time I saw her in cleats."

"Hmm. Didn't notice." I shrug and try to sound nonchalant. "Maybe she thought they went with her outfit." Inside I am freaking out. The idea of the real Cait liking Scooter is disturbing on two levels. First off, I don't even want to think what life would be like if Cait and I liked the same guy. Second off, if Olive can tell I am all stupid over Scooter when I am Cait, that means *he* can probably tell, too. What if this liking-boys thing is turning me into a ditz?

Thankfully, she changes the subject before I can put my foot in my mouth.

"Oh, I forgot to ask, you don't mind reading Danny, do you?"

"No problem," I say, even though I have no idea what she's talking about. I will read to Danny until the cows come home if we can just stop talking about Scooter. It makes my mind all wiggy.

"Great." Olive grins at me and goes back to her homework. I guess I said the right thing.

I stare at my own paper, wishing I could tell Olive the truth. I'd really like to tell her how easy fractions seem now, but that would seem lame. And I'm dying to tell her about my crush on Scooter, and how cool it was teaching him to do

90

headers at lunch. Only that's out of the question because, for better or worse, that wasn't actually me. And if Olive knew we were switching after we promised never to fool her? Well, I might just lose my best friend.

CHAPTER ELEVEN

♪ Caitlin ♩

I am changing my clothes so many times these days I'm starting to feel like a runway model — well, except for the gym clothes. The second I emerge from the gym bathroom stall in my street clothes (and cleats?!) I have to walk around the corner to my locker and put on my *gym* clothes. My heart is hammering because I feel like we barely pulled off our little lunch switch, and Andie had to walk right past Maddie on her way out of the locker room! Luckily, she was still pulling on her sweatshirt, so Maddie didn't even notice her.

"Hey, Cait. Where were you at lunch? I was waiting and waiting. I even got you the last strawberry yogurt, but then when you didn't show up I ate it."

"Sorry, I —" I start to explain, but Maddie just keeps talking, twirling one of her curls. And I am especially grateful for her gift of gab.

"I looked for you by the band room, but Mr. Kolb saw me and asked if I had a minute to go over 'The Star Spangled Banner' since we're going to play it at sporting events this season. And I couldn't say no. I mean, it was Mr. Kolb! And then once we started, Sam showed up and we did it all over again." Maddie stops talking just long enough to take a breath, then adds, "So, where were you?"

For a second I am not sure what to say. If I tell her I was playing soccer it is going to sound weird. And what if she takes it the wrong way and thinks I'm avoiding her? Or that I am not a bona fide band kid anymore? But what else can I say? I'm pretty sure that people saw "me" on the field.

"I, uh, was doing some extra credit for gym," I stammer.

"Well, that explains the cleats," Maddie says, giving my footwear a funny look. She opens her locker, looking a little miffed, and babbles about how they could have used me to go over the band number. I futilely will myself not to blush while I finish changing. I feel totally weird lying to her.

"Sorry," I say. And I mean it.

"So we heard your sister won the Mathletic competition." TarandIvy zoom into our row of lockers and sit down on the benches. It takes me a second to realize they are talking to me. They hardly *ever* talk to me.

"Is this something you put her up to?" Tara adds, running her hand through her short hair and looking at me expectantly.

Maddie looks from TarandIvy to me and back. She doesn't say anything, which is worrisome. And I can't think of a thing to say, either.

"Uh, yeah, I kind of dared her."

TarandIvy bob their heads in unison. "Yeah, it didn't exactly strike us as something Andie would choose to do," Ivy says. "Kind of like you playing soccer."

As fast as I can, I redirect the conversation. "You know Andie. She can never back down from a dare." My giggle sounds nervous even to me. "Besides, she needs all the extra credit she can get," I add, hoping they're buying it.

Tara shrugs. "Probably couldn't hurt," she says, and cocks an eyebrow at me. "Is that why you were playing soccer with Scooter? To get extra credit?" With that she and Ivy saunter out to the gym for roll call, leaving Maddie and me alone in the locker room. Maddie's silence is deafening.

As soon as I am dressed, we walk wordlessly to the bleachers. I know Maddie is thinking about what they said about me playing soccer with Scooter. It isn't like me. But what can I say? I still can't speak. In fact, I have no idea how I am going to find my voice in time to shout, "Here," when the Tank takes attendance.

"Is there something you want to tell me?" Maddie finally asks.

I wish I could scream yes and spill the whole story. Maddie is not acting mad, but she is obviously upset, and it seems wrong to trick her this way. I am wondering what would make her angrier — tricking her or lying to her about tricking her — when things get even worse.

"Hey, there you are!" Scooter jogs up to me, smiling all lopsided. He waves at Maddie, who stares back at him blankly and remains disturbingly quiet.

"I can't wait to show my brother my new header." Scooter grins. "Thanks for the lesson."

I feel a lame smile plastered on my face as I look from Scooter to Maddie. "Anytime." I shrug, hoping nobody asks for a demo.

Maddie just stares. Her silence is really creeping me out. Finally, after roll call, during our three warm-up laps, Maddie says, "Don't worry. I get it."

"Get what?" I ask.

"You like him," she says. "That's why you blew me off. You know, you can tell me that kind of stuff, Cait. I'll understand." Maddie has a wounded look, and she picks up her pace so she is running a little ahead.

Distracted, I try to speed up a bit and stumble. The knot in my stomach must be a rock, because I suddenly feel heavy. And caught.

I can't explain anything to Maddie until I can talk to Andie. I don't want to screw things up for her. But if I'm not careful, this whole switcheroo is going to cost me my best friend!

To make matters worse, Scooter keeps stealing glances in my direction. And he is smiling way too much.

When the warm-ups are over, Coach Tangara tells us that since we all passed the fitness evaluation we can have free play this period. I feel Scooter's eyes on me as he heads for a soccer ball.

Oh no. I grab Maddie by the hand. "Wanna play volleyball?" I ask, hoping she can forgive me. Hoping my eyes tell her how sorry I am since my mouth can't seem to.

"Why not?" Maddie agrees with a feeble smile. "If you're sure you don't want to play soccer. . . ." She nods toward Scooter, who is beelining for us.

"I would rather play with you," I say honestly.

Maddie smiles, for real this time, then picks up a ball and tosses it to me.

I attempt to tap it back. It jams my little finger, but I try not to wince as Maddie scrambles after the ball.

"Cait!" Suddenly, Scooter is right there. "Don't you want to get back on the field?" He looks at me expectantly.

"I don't mind," Maddie says, walking back up with the volleyball under her arm.

"Nah," I brush Scooter off, hoping I'm not ruining anything for my sister. "Volleyball season is coming up, I need to work on some other skills." I shrug, hoping I sound suitably jockish.

Scooter looks bummed, the way your dog looks when you're leaving for school and she was hoping for a walk. Maddie looks stunned. Like I just demonstrated my ability to change colors or something. But thankfully, Scooter gets the message and walks away.

"Okay. Maybe next time," he says over his shoulder.

"Volleyball skills, huh?" Maddie says, looking

at me sideways and bumping the ball to me. I drop it and run after it lamely.

"You can see I need the practice," I joke.

"Are you really thinking of going out for the team? My mom wishes I would try out for more sports. I told her band takes too much time, but she doesn't believe me. I mean, I never really thought of you as the volleyball type. Or any sports type, actually. But maybe you and Andie are more alike than I thought."

I sigh, relieved to hear Maddie sounding like her old self. She and I take up position on either side of the volleyball court at the far end of the soccer field. She keeps rattling on while she serves to me. I am so thrilled to be feeling halfway normal I forget to think about what my arms and legs and fingers and toes are doing and return the ball easily. Maddie sends it back to me, and I jump and spike it. The ball shoots straight down, bouncing behind Maddie.

"Good one!"

I can hardly believe I made an actual play. Maybe Andie and I are more alike than *I* thought, too.

CHAPTER TWELVE

⚽ ANDiE ⚽

You would think, living in the same house and all, that it wouldn't be hard to find a minute over a weekend to talk to your own sister. But somehow Sunday night arrived without Caitlin and me having had a single real conversation.

The whole weekend was a blur. Friday night I had a sleepover at Tara's. It was her birthday, and she and Ivy and their moms set up this weekend-long soccer clinic to celebrate. It was totally over the top and awesome.

We ate, slept, and breathed soccer for two days straight. Tara's mom was so into it she even made this huge tray of spaghetti sprinkled with parsley to look like a soccer field, with, you guessed it, soccer meatballs. We drank soda out of orange cones with straws in the tops, watched *Bend It Like Beckham*, and talked almost all night. Then we ran drills all day Saturday.

Saturday night we slept at Ivy's house — and this time we really slept. In the morning Ivy's dad took us in their minivan to a major league soccer game! It was so exciting I couldn't stay in my seat. It was the first professional soccer game any of us had been to.

Tara, Ivy, and I were screaming the whole time. We even got the wave started once, and watched it go all the way around the stadium three times! The only part that wasn't perfect was that Olive wasn't there. She had a Bruger family reunion and said she would try to see the game on ESPN from her uncle's house where they were.

The weekend was so great and so crazy that I forgot all about telling Cait that I had made more plans with Scooter for after school on Monday, and that I had to borrow her identity yet again. In fact, I almost forgot all about Scooter until Sunday night.

Once, on Friday when we stopped the movie to make more popcorn, Tara said, "Maybe we should have invited Caitlin, too."

"She sure is more interested in soccer lately," Ivy agreed.

I took a big swig of soda. Then Tara said, "Or is it Scooter she's interested in?" Holy crud. I nearly shot Dr. Pepper out of my nose at that one. I had no idea what to say, so I quickly went to the bathroom.

Now, home at last, I am totally wiped and ready to hit the sack. But before Monday morning arrives I need to talk to Cait. I walk slowly down the hall to knock on her door. Inside I can hear her practicing her clarinet. Then I hear something else. Maddie is over, coaching Cait and talking a mile a minute. There's not much I can say in front of Maddie, so I decide not to bug them and call Olive to give her the blow-by-blow instead.

"It was amazing," I tell her. "The Galaxy won by two goals, and the second half was intense. Next time we have to see a WUSA game." The guys' games are okay, but a women's game would rock.

"I wish I could have been there!" Olive says enviously.

I wish she could have been there, too. I have to fight a sudden urge to tell her about Scooter, and Caitlin, and everything. I stop myself because if I don't I won't be able to tell her another thing in my whole life. She would be that mad. So after a while I say good-bye and hang up without mentioning any of it.

Halfway through Monday I realize I still haven't told Cait I need to be her after school so I can run drills with Scooter.

I briefly consider showing up as me — the real Andie — to play. For one thing, I really want to tell him about the amazing goal the Galaxy scored when one of the guys headed in a ball kicked from midfield. And for another, I am dying to know if Scooter would want to play with *me*. If I'm not Cait, I mean.

But I'm also afraid. I'm afraid he just likes me when I'm Cait. After all, Cait is the one he asked to meet him after school. Cait is so much more laidback around him than I would be. I mean, in a weird way, I like myself better when I am Cait. I can relax; I don't have to prove anything.

The whole thing makes my head hurt.

Olive blows the wrapper off her straw and it hits me in the forehead. "Earth to Andie," she drones in an alien voice. "Do you read me?"

"Yeah, sorry. What were you saying?" I ask. I pop another Tater Tot into my mouth and scan the cafeteria for Caitlin.

"I *said* I didn't get any time to practice lines all weekend, so I hope you're ready."

"I'm ready for anything," I answer, distracted. Cait is nowhere, and I'm starting to worry that she has plans — plans that might require her to be herself — and I might *have* to meet Scooter as Andie so there aren't two Caitlins running around. Just thinking about that makes the Tater Tots that are already in my stomach start to churn.

"Did you sleep at *all* this weekend?"

Olive is looking at me very suspiciously. I guess I'm ignoring her again.

"Sorry!" I cover my mouth, hiding a fake yawn. Exhaustion is a great excuse. And when you're having an identity crisis, you need every excuse you can come up with.

"So, for the audition, I think Sandy's best scene is when she and Frenchy talk after the race. And Rizzo's best is right before she sings 'Sandra Dee,' don't you think?"

I can't think. I just nod.

"And don't worry. I have two scripts in my locker."

Why does she need two? I am not following at all but I keep nodding. Just before the five-minute bell I run down to see if I can catch Cait on her way to gym. I hang out by her locker as long as I can, but then Tara and Ivy come in, still on fire from our weekend. If I stay any longer I'll be late. Mr. Mosely likes me now and I'd like to keep it that way.

103

Quickly, I dial the combo on Cait's locker (it's our birth date — hard to forget!) and pull out the extra gym bag she keeps in there. I'll need her clothes, and figure it's safer to get them now in case I don't have time to get them after school. "Tell Cait I needed to borrow some clothes, 'kay?" I yell to Tara and Ivy, and then I hustle to class.

The fractions are a little harder today, but I do my best to pay attention, go slow, and write everything out. It helps. But it's not easy with Olive humming *Grease* songs the whole time.

The break before eighth period is my final chance to find my sister. But Cait is nowhere to be found, so when the last bell rings at the end of the day I change into her cleats, shorts, and T-shirt, cross my fingers, and jog up the hill behind the gym toward the field.

Scooter is already waiting. The sun glints off his hair and suddenly I'm sure that I am doing the right thing. I jog faster, feeling my ponytail bounce. Oops! At the last second I remember to let my hair down. Fortunately, Scooter was looking the other way.

CHAPTER THIRTEEN
♪ CAITLIN ♪

On Monday, after working with Maddie all weekend on our pieces for Jazz Ensemble auditions, I feel pretty great. It was so fantastic to get in all that rehearsal time. I actually feel like myself again. The only bit of Andie I still possess is a sliver of her self-confidence, which I think I'll try to hold on to.

Maddie is totally ready, too, even though she doesn't know it yet. She's nervous. I know, because when she's anxious she talks even more than usual, and a whole lot faster. Last night she was yammering at the speed of light. She talked so fast she started to sound like a cartoon mouse, or a kid sucking helium balloons at a birthday party. I started to worry she would hyperventilate and tried to remind her to breathe.

Maddie's audition piece is this great Dixieland number. It's unusual, up-tempo, and catchy. But sometimes, when her nerves get to her, she speeds it up too much, which is not good since jazz is all about timing.

Last night we decided we should meet after school today in the band room, where Mr. Kolb is holding tryouts. If we practice in there we can get used to the acoustics. Then maybe we won't be so nervous about the new surroundings and the people listening during auditions tomorrow.

Taking my time, I watch the other kids clear out of school for the day. I swing by my locker, shove my clarinet into my book bag, and haul it toward the band room. Then as I'm walking past the girls' bathroom I hear something weird. Something snuffly.

For some reason I decide to investigate. If it's a plumbing issue I can always back away slowly, right? I push open the door and what I see makes me feel like I've been punched in the gut.

It's Olive. She's sitting hunched over in one of the stalls with the door half open. Her face is hidden, but it's clear that she's crying.

In an instant I know why, and that it is all my fault.

In my jazz haze I completely forgot to tell Andie

that I made a date for her to run lines with Olive today after school. Poor Olive! With her family thing this weekend she probably hasn't had a second to practice. Her auditions are tomorrow, like mine. She barely has any rehearsal time left, and she thinks Andie, her best friend, is standing her up!

I back out as quietly as I can and run down to Andie's gym locker to tell her she needs to go help Olive. But I don't see my sister anywhere.

I squeeze my eyes shut for a second, knowing I am out of options. Olive needs Andie. And there are only two people who will do. Luckily, I know my sister's locker combo (it's our birth date, backward). I pull out some soccer clothes, the only thing that's in there, change into Andie, and haul all my gear back to Olive in the other bathroom.

"Oh, there you are!" I breeze in. "I've been looking all over for you!"

Olive lifts her head off her knees and wipes her tears. She has funny imprints around her eyes, but I don't say anything.

"I thought you forgot," she sniffs.

"Forgot?" I repeat, pretending to be shocked. "No way."

Olive smiles blearily. "Guess I'm being dramatic."

I laugh and give her a hug. "That's why we're here, right?"

Olive shrugs. "Yeah. It's just that I feel like I already lost your sister, you know? It would be terrible if you stopped liking me, too. And you've been so distracted lately. I kind of felt like you were avoiding me."

I can't believe my ears. Olive feels like she lost me? I have to blink back my own tears. And I want to shout at Olive, *"I like you!"* But I can't blow my cover and have her think Andie and I have been tricking her. That would mess *everything* up, because then *none* of us would be friends.

"You know, Caitlin really does like you," I tell her. "She just hasn't been herself lately."

Olive sniffs again and emerges from the stall. "I'm just glad you remembered." She sighs, looks at her blotchy, tearstained face in the mirror, and checks her profile. "You know? Maybe I should think about trying out for Frenchy. She's kind of tragic."

"Yeah, but all those wigs? Frenchy changes hair color, like, nine times. Besides, you're leading-lady material."

Olive shines like a star at the compliment, and I can tell she's back. "You ready?" She glances down at all the stuff I am carrying. Her eyes linger on the clarinet case sticking out of my bag.

"I'm, uh, taking it home for Cait." I shrug. She grabs one of the straps and we walk down to the multipurpose room lugging the stuff between us.

Olive wants to practice on the stage so she can be sure she is projecting enough to reach the back of the house. Just like I want to do with Maddie in the band room. Oh no. Maddie! I nearly forgot about her.

I feel panic rising again and hope Maddie is practicing without me. I feel torn. Being two people with two best friends is too much. No matter where I am or what I am doing I am letting someone down. But right now it seems like Olive is the one who needs me — uh, Andie — more. Maybe Andie and I should have been quadruplets, I think.

Being worried about Olive (and Maddie) takes my mind off how much I despise acting. It also helps that the room is basically empty — Ms. Roper, the acting teacher, is busy with the set builders. And it turns out that running lines isn't as horrible as I thought. By the end I have to admit that I am getting into it!

Pretending to be Andie is fun. But pretending to be Andie being Danny is even better. I roll up my T-shirt sleeves, stick my lips out in a pout, and do my best John Travolta imitation. "Oh, Sandy."

Olive is on the floor laughing and begging me to try out, too, when Andie walks in — the real Andie.

Only *I'm* supposed to be Andie.

My heart flies into my throat and I try to think of a way to signal to Andie that I am being her. I make my eyes really big and try to wave her back out of the room. Luckily, she gets it. (Thank goodness for that twin thing!) And, thank goodness, her hair is already down and she's wearing gym clothes that look like mine.

Before I can think to wonder *why* she is dressed in clothes that actually match she calls out loudly, "Hey, Andie! I've been looking all over for you. Mom's waiting outside." I look at the clock at the back of the auditorium and groan inwardly. Practice hour is long over. We were supposed to meet Mom by the curb ages ago.

"Olive, you want a ride?" the real Andie asks.

"That'd be great." Olive gathers her scripts and bag. She waves to Ms. Roper, and I shoot Andie a look. Was that a good idea? I ask with my eyes. Now we have to stay switched in front of Mom, the one person we can't fool, the person who busted us the last time!

"It'll be fine. We'll be sitting in the back," Andie whispers as I brush past her. "She'll never know."

All I can do is hope that she's right as Olive, Andie, and I pile into the backseat.

"Look, it's my triplets!" Mom says, glancing in her rearview mirror.

It would be fun that the three of us are together again if I weren't so tense. Thankfully, Olive breaks into "We Go Together," and Andie and I join in on the "rama lama ding dong"s. We sing as loud and as badly as we can, cracking ourselves up after the "we'll always be together" part. For a second it really feels like old times.

But when the song ends Mom tells Andie, "Your hair looks nice down, sweetie."

Olive bends over to get her bag and Andie shoots me a look behind her back. Olive doesn't say anything, but when we drop her off in front of her house I swear she studies us until we pull away.

At home I try to push the whole thing out of my mind. I head straight for my room and start in on my jazz piece. Only I keep messing up. The improvised bit at the end is hard because you have to make it sound easy. And the harder I try, the worse it sounds.

I had it this morning! What happened? It's like I'm forgetting who I am with all of this switching and pretending. I can't even tell who I *want* to be anymore — me, or my sister.

I blow as hard as I can into my clarinet and it makes a noise that could make your ears bleed. It's terrible, but that's exactly how I feel.

Andie comes in and flops onto my bed. She looks pretty bad, too. "Sorry I had to be you again today," she says.

"Sorry I had to be you, too."

"I forgot I made plans with Scooter. I should have just told him I was busy, I mean, that you had plans, but . . ."

I nod. "It's complicated."

I sink down next to her and we both stare up at my ceiling. It is dotted with those green glow-in-the-dark star stickers Andie and I put up with Dad years ago. Some of them are in constellation formation. We were going to make the whole sky, but after a while we got bored and just stuck them on wherever. I can still pick out Orion, though. It feels like his arrow is aimed at me.

"I mean, I get why you did it." I sigh.

"You do?"

"Yeah. I think it's easier to be someone else

112

sometimes. You don't have to worry so much about what people will think . . ."

"Because it isn't you!" Andie finishes.

Boy, is that the truth. "Know what?" I ask my twin. "As hard as it is to keep switching . . ."

"It's going to be even harder to stop," she finishes for both of us.

Maybe it would be easier if Orion just shot me right now.

CHAPTER FOURTEEN

⚽ ANDiE ⚽

"Stop looking so stressed!" Tara tells me when I walk into homeroom on Tuesday. I had no idea I was looking stressed, but I must be, 'cause Ivy notices, too.

"Yeah." She rubs my shoulders. "We have nothing to worry about. We'll be first-string even if we are seventh graders. We're that good."

I force a smile. "We totally are!" I agree. I guess we all have tryouts on the brain, but for different reasons. It isn't making the team that has me worried, it's who'll be watching. The last thing Scooter said to me when we ran drills was that he would come watch tryouts for the girls. But guess who he's expecting to see try out?

I feel a little ill just thinking about it. In some ways I am so ready to be myself again — all the time. Trying out as Cait and being Cait on the team would be a disaster. So that's out. But what's in?

I sit down, drop my head onto my desk, and exhale. When this whole switch thing started it sounded simple. I had no idea it would turn into such a sticky mess.

Ivy flips her braid onto her back and takes a seat next to Tara. And while our teacher calls roll I try to think of ways to keep Scooter away from tryouts. I could drop something really heavy on his toe so he has to go to the doctor, but then we couldn't play soccer together anymore, at least not for a while. Maybe I could call his mom pretending I am the school nurse and ask her to come get him. Only as soon as she arrives she would see he is fine. I mull this over some more.

Then, right before the bell, it comes to me. I can try out twice. That way I can make sure that *I* make the team, and that *Cait* doesn't. Then all I have to do is get the real Cait to blow Scooter off while I dazzle him with my moves. Transfer his interest, and voilà! Simple, right?

Wrong. Even in my stressed-out state I recognize that the plan is wacky, not to mention complicated. But it's the only idea I have.

I glance over at Olive, who hasn't even said hello. She is bent over some papers on her desk, and when I punch her lightly on the arm she barely looks up.

"Hey," she mumbles. "I almost have this by heart. I really want to be able to do it without the script."

I look at the pages on her desk. It's her *Grease* script. She is studying her lines like her life depends on it.

"Are tryouts today?" I ask. She shoots me a look. They must be. And she must have already told me that nine million times . . . only I don't remember.

"I wish I could watch," I tell her.

"Yeah, it's too bad you and Cait have got your own tryouts to do," she says. Is it me, or does her smile look a little forced? "You'd be so great in the show. I think you're both natural actresses." She bends back over her script and I just stand there turning pink. I can feel the color start at my ears and move in toward my nose until my whole face is hot. Olive knows.

I wish I could run upstairs to Cait's homeroom and pull her down here so we could come clean together. I feel awful, because now both Olive and I know I have broken my promise never to fool her again — only Olive doesn't know why, and I'm sure she'd understand.

116

Scanning the room, I search for a private corner to pull Olive into and explain. But Tara and Ivy are right there. And it doesn't really matter, because I need to talk to Cait before I can talk to Olive. We promised.

I bite my lips together and wish that Olive could read my mind so I could tell her without actually telling her. She doesn't even look at me as she hands her extra script to Tara and asks if she will read Danny. In fact, she doesn't look at me for the rest of the day.

At lunch I search for Cait so I can tell her about my plan for soccer tryouts, and more important, about Olive. Her annoyance is no act. She must think we're pulling a prank just for fun, and secret or no, it's time to come clean and apologize. Only Cait is nowhere to be found.

I spot Maddie in the cafeteria and hurry over. "Have you seen Cait?" I ask.

"No. I thought maybe you knew where she disappeared to. It was, like, she was in homeroom, and then, poof. Gone. She's been doing that a lot lately. I hope she's not nervous about tryouts. I mean, what if she's barfing or something? Maybe I should check the bathrooms. Or maybe she's in the library. You know, sometimes she likes to read to take her mind off of stuff. Then again, she might have gone to the band room. I am heading over there as soon as I eat my yogurt —"

I cut Maddie off. "Just let her know I'm looking for her?" I ask. Then I walk away before she can start talking again.

By the time school is out the knot in my stomach is the size of a grapefruit and I know all I can do is just go on with my plan and hope for the best. With Cait gone and Olive mad, I figure things can't get much worse.

That's where I'm wrong.

Feeling sorry for myself, I grab Caitlin's giant gym bag out of her locker and carry it to the upstairs bathroom to change into Caitlin's soccer clothes in private. I don't want Tara and Ivy, who will be in the gym any second to get ready themselves, getting suspicious. The last thing I need is to make them angry, too.

I tug out my ponytail holder, step into a stall, and take a breath. I can do this. But when I open Cait's bag the first thing I see is her clarinet case. I have Cait's clarinet, and Jazz Ensemble tryouts are happening any second! For all I know they have already started.

I slap my hand over my eyes and realize what I need to do. I grab the case and race out of the bathroom. This whole crazy switch started so Cait could get into Jazz Ensemble. If I don't get her instrument to her, then it will all have been for nothing. I will have lost my best friend, a cute boy, and my mind, for nothing.

bathroom. This whole draw-sqw-swarped no OJ,
to rip the intestine is insatiable. If I don't get her
instrument to her, there it will all have been for
nothing. I will have had my best friend a cold face,
and I'm filled for nothing.

CHAPTER FIFTEEN

♪ Caitlin ♪

Tuesday is like torture. I am so nervous about Jazz Ensemble auditions I can barely stand it. And Maddie is not helping. She just goes on and on about Mr. Kolb and what a perfectionist he is. Apparently, he walked in on her practicing (without me) yesterday and gave her a few pointers.

"I was totally wigged out at first," she babbles. "I mean, he was being super-picky! But then I started doing what he was telling me to do, and my playing got better. A *lot* better! I even kept things in tempo! I'm telling you, Caitlin, that man is a genius! He could turn anyone into a musician. Well, not anyone, I suppose, but you know what I mean!"

Whew! Maddie's musical progress seems to be making her mouth more out of control than ever. I end up tuning her out until the period starts. I can feel my blood pressure rise all through homeroom.

I spend all of lunch in the library with my headphones on. A part of me wants to practice, but my first clarinet teacher always told me you have to take a break, to let your mind and fingers rest and allow the music to become part of you. I thought it was pretty lame at the time, but now I see that there is such a thing as too much practice. So instead of actually playing I just picture myself playing.

All the way to the band room after school I play my audition piece in my head, but even in my head the ending sounds wrong. I try to hear it right. Smooth. Easy. But all I can hear is my own voice yelling, "I am going to mess up!"

Suddenly, I wish Maddie were with me so she could drown out my nagging inner voice. I wish Andie were with me to tell me to "knock 'em dead." And I wish Olive were with me to help me act the part of a great musician. I head for the locker room, where I stashed my clarinet because it crowds my books so much. Clothes are lying around from the people at athletic tryouts. I glance around for Andie so I can wish her luck (not that she needs it) and hope that maybe she could rub a little luck off on me.

There are a few girls still changing, but no Andie. I dial the combo of my locker, trying to reassure myself that it will all be fine. I can do this by myself, as myself. Mom and Dad must have given me at least a little bit of Andie's confidence. . . .

You can do this! I tell myself. Only I need my clarinet. My bag is gone.

My bag is gone?

Get it together, I scold myself. I must not have put my clarinet in here like I thought. And now I am going to be late. I run back into the hall, willing myself not to freak out.

"Hey!" a voice pulls me out of my head. I turn around and find myself looking right at Scooter Vanderhoff. "Shouldn't you be changing? Where are your cleats?" he asks, looking down at my skirt and flats. "The Tank is on the field. Tryouts are starting and they're doing seventh graders first!"

"I know." I gulp. But we are not thinking about the same tryouts. Scooter is expecting me to go out for the soccer team. And if I tell him the truth — that I couldn't care less about Andie's favorite sport — I will completely blow it for Andie.

I am frozen, once again.

"You better hurry," he says. "Coach is waiting for you."

Just the thought gives me chills. "For me?" I ask lamely. "Really?"

Scooter gives me an exasperated look. "Have you blocked one too many shots with your head?" He grabs me by the arm and starts pulling me through the gym and out toward the field. "Just come on. I'm sure you can make the team without cleats."

I am too stunned to pull away. When we get close to the sideline, TarandIvy spot us and come running over.

"We'll take it from here," Tara tells Scooter.

The poor guy raises his hands as if in defeat. "All right," he says a little nervously before jogging over to the coach.

As soon as Scooter is gone TarandIvy turn to me, all business. They study my face in silence and then ask in unison, "All right, where's Andie?"

Good question.

"I don't know. I - I thought she was with you," I stammer.

"A likely story." They are staring at me so hard I get a little nervous.

"I'm sure she'll be here in a minute," I mumble. "She would never miss soccer tryouts."

Their eyes glint, and Ivy smiles. "You're right. Andie would never miss tryouts."

"In fact," Tara says, smiling back at Ivy, "I think *Andie* is here already."

CHAPTER SIXTEEN

⚽ ANDiE ⚽

By the time I get to the band room my lungs are about to burst. At least all this running around will have me warmed up for soccer tryouts since I am definitely going to miss the regular warm-up. I slow my pace, breathing hard, and peek into the window in the door to search for Caitlin. I don't see her right off, but the band teacher, Mr. Kolb, sees me. He scowls, walks over, and sticks his head out the door.

I am about to shove the case into his hand, tell him it's for Cait, and take off, but he grasps me gently by the arm before I can do anything.

"What are you doing out here in the hall?" he asks. "We've been waiting for you inside."

I start to protest, but I'm still trying to catch

my breath. Plus he's not hearing it and he has my arm. I have no choice but to follow him inside.

He pulls me into the room and plants me front and center before a surprisingly large audience.

About sixty kids, all holding instruments, are staring at me expectantly. Not sure what to do, I hold up one hand in a wave while I scan the crowd. Not one of them is my twin. But then it occurs to me a crowd this big might be the reason why she's not here. Just the idea of performing in front of so many people might make Cait lose her lunch. My poor sister is probably heaving her guts out in a stall down the hall right now!

Just thinking about that doubles my panic. I want to run and find her so I can help *her* find her nerve. But I need to stall, to give her a chance to get here on her own. I just keep thinking, Please, don't let this all have been for nothing!

"We're ready when you are, Caitlin," Mr. Kolb says. He has not taken his eyes off of me, and he definitely sounds annoyed.

I feel numb. Maddie stands up and takes the clarinet case out of my hand. She opens it and puts the clarinet together, squinting at me. "Where have you been? Are you okay? You look weird," she whispers.

"You have no idea," I mutter. I take the clarinet and look at Mr. Kolb. "Um, can I go last?" I ask.

"You *are* last," Mr. Kolb says, cocking an eyebrow. "Even the eighth graders have auditioned." I look toward the door hoping for a miracle, but there's no one there. I can't let Cait miss tryouts. Luckily, I have had some music lessons. Not many, but . . .

"Come on, you know how to do this," Maddie whispers. She forces a piece of sheet music into my hand. "Just don't think too much." Okay . . .

Maddie positions my music stand and puts the sheet music on it, not that I can read a note! I stare at all those little black dots and lines on the page wondering that the heck they are trying to tell me. Time for plan B.

"Um, Mr. Kolb? I think I would like to . . . improvise," I say, hoping that's the right word. It sounds jazzy enough.

Mr. Kolb nods and says, "That's fine, we'd just like you to do *something*."

I swallow and put the reed into my mouth. This can't be that hard. Just put your lips together and blow, right? So I do.

A horrible screeching, squawking noise erupts from the clarinet. Everyone grimaces. Even me.

I take the clarinet out of my mouth and look at it. Did I do that? Maybe I broke it while I was running over here. I try again. It seems better this time — not quite as bad as the cow-sitting-on-a-duck noise I made the first time. But the expressions on people's faces tell me this is not going well.

Every person in the room looks like they are listening to fingernails screeching down a chalkboard, or maybe smelling fish that's been sitting in the sun. Even Maddie looks disgusted. But I have to go on. What else can I do? I close my eyes and play the only song Cait has ever taught me. And by the end I am actually hitting the notes, kind of.

When I toot my last note and lower the clarinet, Maddie's mouth is open so wide I can see her gum. I had been hoping for a little applause, but I am met with stunned silence. Was I that bad?

I turn to Mr. Kolb, hoping to see a smile on *his* face, at least. I was improvising. I was innovating. Maybe he will be impressed.

Or not.

Mr. Kolb blinks rapidly. He removes his glasses and wipes the lenses with his shirttail before rubbing his eyes and putting them back on.

"That was . . . interesting," Mr. Kolb says.

"Interesting" is another word for "bad" in the teachers' dictionary of student-friendly insults.

"'Twinkle, Twinkle' is a bold choice for a jazz band audition," he goes on. He looks out at the rest of the kids. "That concludes our Ensemble tryouts. I will post a list of the musicians who have been accepted tomorrow."

I slap a hand up over my own gaping mouth. Kolb does not have to say aloud that I didn't make Jazz Ensemble — that *Cait* didn't make Jazz Ensemble. And there is no need to wait and read it on a piece of paper tomorrow. Here I am, trying desperately to get her in, and instead I may have tainted her whole junior high musical career with my "interesting" audition.

I want to screech like the clarinet, but I won't give up so easily. As the other students file out I shuffle closer to Mr. Kolb. "I'm sorry," I say softly. "It must be nerves."

"I'm sorry, too," he says slowly. "I had much higher expectations of you, Ms. Kline."

"If I could just try again. Maybe t-tomorrow . . ." I stammer.

Mr. Kolb shakes his head and clucks his tongue. "There's always next year," he says, brushing me off, and confirming what I already knew in my heart. Cait didn't get into Jazz Ensemble, and it is all my fault.

CHAPTER SEVENTEEN
♪ Caitlin ♪

The next thing I know I'm back in the locker room with TarandIvy, who are transforming me into a soccer player. And in case it's not clear, this is not an easy transformation without my wonder twin.

"Put this on," Tara says, handing me one of her extra jerseys. I pull the purple nylon shirt over my head just as Ivy retrieves a pair of cleats from her seemingly bottomless gym bag.

"You wear the same size shoe as Andie, right?" she asks.

I nod as Ivy unearths shin guards and thrusts them in my direction.

Suddenly, Tara is behind me brushing my hair back and pulling it into a tight ponytail. I glance up at the mirror in front of me and feel a wave of panic.

"I can't do this!" I protest. "I can't be Andie!" TarandIvy exchange a look in the mirror, a look that says, "Yeah, right."

"Of course you can — you've been doing it since school started." Ivy's brown eyes twinkle. She knows. Which means Tara knows, too. Stunned, I watch my reflection turn red and begin to babble maniacally.

"But that was so Andie could be athletic when I couldn't!" I protest, feeling like a weasel that's been caught stealing an egg from a bird's nest. I'm not usually a deceitful person!

Ivy meets my gaze in the mirror. "You mean when you *wouldn't*," she corrects. "You can do this, Caitlin. You're actually a lot more athletic than you think."

"You *have* to do this for your sister," Tara insists. "I don't know where Andie is, but she's got to make the team. We need her."

Oh great, I think miserably. No pressure.

Ivy double knots my cleats and untucks my jersey. Then she stands behind me, puts her hands on my shoulders, and looks at me in the mirror. I swallow and try to look like my sister — confident and sporty. I can't tell if I'm pulling it off, but there's no backing out now.

"Ready?" Tara asks.

Desperately wishing I could tell the truth, I just nod. She pulls me by the arm and we head out the door. I force myself to look straight in front of me as I walk. TarandIvy are so close to me that our shoulders are almost touching, and our footsteps are in sync.

Breathe, I tell myself. As I exhale I realize that as long as I'm standing in between these two girls I'm not alone, and *that* makes me feel stronger. I almost feel like Andie, like a real soccer player. Almost.

"Don't overthink," Tara instructs in a low, serious voice.

"We'll get you the ball. All you have to do is tap it into the net," Ivy adds.

"Keep moving."

"Focus on the ball . . ."

"Not your feet."

"We're ready," they say in unison when we reach the sidelines.

Coach Tangara looks us over and her steely gray eyes rest on my face for what feels like forever. "Where's your sister?" she asks.

I can feel my face getting red yet again — does Andie ever have this problem? — and I try not to flip out. Who does she mean? I wonder as my heart begins to pound even faster. I'm sure everyone within fifty yards can hear it thudding away.

"Caitlin decided to go out for Jazz Ensemble instead," Tara explains easily. "She's been playing the clarinet forever and her improv rocks."

"It does?" I blurt, totally flattered. I never even knew they noticed my music, much less think it rocks.

"Totally," Ivy agrees. "But you know that already, since Caitlin's your sister," she adds.

Out of the corner of my eye I see Scooter's head jerk up at the mention of Caitlin's name, and he looks right at me. He stares at me in this confused way, like I'm somebody familiar he just can't place. I'm pretty sure he knows I'm not the twin he's been hanging out with, but of course I can't be totally sure. Thank goodness he doesn't say anything.

"Jazz Ensemble," Coach Tangara mutters under her breath. My stomach flips as I realize what's happening — I am missing the auditions! They started right after school and are probably over by now! Part of me wants to cut and run — in case there's still a chance — but my feet won't move. The Tank scares the spit out of me, so I just stand there, my mouth as dry as toast. I'm going to see this crazy soccer thing through, for Andie. Making this team is as important to her as Jazz Ensemble is — or was — to me. And I know she would do the same.

I try to pay attention while Coach Tangara lays out the plan for the tryouts — a warm-up, some drills, and a couple of scrimmages. I guess since I've been watching Andie play soccer for years, I actually understand what she's saying. But doing what she asks is a little — okay, a lot — trickier.

Halfway through the warm-up laps I pull a Caitlin. One of my feet goes down wrong, and in trying to right myself I practically wrap my right leg around my left. I drop like a two-ton pretzel and land on both knees. Well, there goes that, I think somberly. Andie's chances blown by my unstoppable klutziness! But before I can even beat myself up TarandIvy are right there with me. They scoop me up by my elbows and for a moment I am practically airborne as they lift me along.

"Move your feet," Tara whispers.

"And stop thinking so much," Ivy says, smiling.

"Just one more lap," Tara encourages.

"You can do it!" Ivy adds.

I scowl at them but keep moving as best I can with my knees smarting. Fortunately, Tangara seems to have missed my whole show. She's looking at her clipboard. Andie still stands a chance as long as nobody tells my feet we're counting on them. . . .

Up ahead I see that Scooter has already finished and is looking back at us. He must think I'm — Andie's — a total loser. I have more to lose for my twin than just a spot on the team. I might just ruin her reputation. The thought makes me cringe, and I stumble again.

"No thinking!" Tara says in singsong.

"This is *fun*!" Ivy crows as we finish the lap. I'm about to collapse on the grass in a heap when Tara elbows me. "Look exhilarated," she whispers. "Tangara is watching us."

The thought of looking exhilarated when I'm feeling like an oaf is so ridiculous I have to laugh. Tara and Ivy grin at me. "That's more like it," they agree together.

Next up are some drills with ball handling, also known as my worst nightmare. Thank goodness TarandIvy are on it, making me look good — or as good as possible — at every turn. Their constant barrage of whispered advice actually makes me forget about falling on my face long enough to dribble the ball instead. And during the scrimmage they guard me and pass me the ball, which gets me more than a few surprisingly decent kicks . . . and even an easy goal!

"Score!" Ivy yells.

"What's with the cheap shot?" Scooter calls from the sidelines, shooting us a suspicious look. But a second later his glower turns into a smirk that I'm pretty sure is directed right at me . . . I mean Andie. "It's not like you need it." I smile back. I haven't destroyed Andie's reputation . . . yet. And Andie is right; Scooter has changed a lot since preschool.

"Andie, incoming!" someone calls out. I look down and see the ball heading toward me, fast. There's no time to think. I take a quick step back and kick it toward the net, hard . . .

And score an honest-to-goodness goal! I can't believe it, but there it is. Maybe TarandIvy are right. Maybe when I don't think about it too much I can actually be a little bit athletic.

But thinking about not thinking gets me thinking. And as if that isn't enough, suddenly the ball is airborne again and flying my way. I know that Andie would tap it in with her head, so I jump up to head it in, Andie-style. Only instead I bash my brain and send it sky-high and out of bounds.

That's when the real Andie jogs up in her real soccer clothes. "Thanks for standing in for me," she says casually, tagging me out.

"What's going on here?" the Tank bellows as she hustles over, looking from me to Andie and back.

Andie straightens her shoulders and fesses up. "Sorry, Coach," Andie says. "I was running late and my sister was trying to cover for me."

"So you're Caitlin?" Coach asks me, confused.

"And I'm Andie," Andie confirms. "The soccer player."

"Then get out there and play," Coach tells my sister, looking a little annoyed. Then she fixes her steely gaze on me again. "You want to try out?" she asks. "No thanks," I reply quickly. I've had enough soccer for one day — or maybe a lifetime. I head to the bench and I sit down near Scooter, who's taking some time out, too. He keeps looking at Andie and then back at me, but he doesn't say anything.

I keep my eyes on Andie, who is rocking the field. She is everywhere, passing, trapping, and kicking. And she is awesome.

Finally, Scooter gets up the nerve to say something. "So you're . . . Caitlin?" he asks.

Just then Andie heads the ball into the corner of the goal.

"Yeah," I say with a confirmatory nod.

"And *that's* Andie," Scooter says, grinning from ear to ear and looking at my sister.

"The one and only," I agree. And thank goodness.

CHAPTER EIGHTEEN

⚽ ANDiE ⚽

I rush up to the ball and give it a tiny backward tap with the heel of my foot, then spin around and move it up the field. A second later I'm just outside the goal and — *thwack!* — I kick it right past the goalie. Man, I love soccer. And I am unbelievably grateful that my sister filled in long enough for me to get here.

I shoot a quick look to the sidelines, where Caitlin is sitting with Scooter, cheering me on. As I watch my sister leap to her feet I am suddenly overwhelmed by a sinking feeling — the realization that she will not be playing in Jazz Ensemble this year, and all because of me. I'm so distracted by that miserable thought that I don't see the ball coming.

"Andie!" Tara and Ivy shout in unison. Too late.

Ooof! The ball hits me right in the gut. I ignore the pain as the ball falls to the grass with a soft thud, pull my leg back, and kick it, hard. It sails up the field right to Ivy, who takes it toward the goal and scores.

Just then Tangara blows the whistle. "That's it, people," she calls. "Nice job all around. I'll be posting the team roster tomorrow morning outside my office."

I jog to the sidelines holding my stomach.

"Way to space out," Scooter teases. "But even better was the way you saved the play," he adds with a grin.

"Are you all right?" Caitlin is on her feet in a second.

I nod. "I'm fine. Believe me, I've had much worse."

"You looked awesome out there," Cait crows, giving me a hug.

My smile disappears in an instant and my stomach suddenly feels way worse, and not because of the hit it took from the soccer ball. I look my sister right in her just-like-mine eyes.

"Thanks again for standing in for me," I say with a gulp. "But I, um, I don't think I did as good a job for you."

I can see Cait's brain processing what I'm saying, and her eyes go wide. "Jazz Ensemble?" she whispers, looking up at me. "You didn't . . ."

"I did," I say.

"And?" She sounds totally breathless, and I can see a flicker of hope in her eyes.

"And I have two left lungs," I say grimly. "I was terrible! I don't know how you make that thing sound good."

Cait sinks onto the bottom bleacher bench to digest the news. "Practice, I guess," she says after what seems like forever.

I bite my lip and slide onto the metal bench next to her. My stomach knots are tightening by the second. "I'm so sorry, Cait," I say quietly. "I thought I was just bringing you your clarinet, and then Mr. Kolb saw me, and thought I was you, and . . . when you weren't there I thought you got scared and . . ." I trail off, feeling miserable. I can tell Caitlin is trying not to look totally devastated, but I know better. Jazz Ensemble was her dream!

"Don't worry," she tells me, smiling as best she can and getting to her feet. "There's always next year."

I look around for Scooter and Tara and Ivy, but

everyone has disappeared. Cait and I are alone as we head to the locker room.

As soon as we walk through the door, Tara looks up from the bench where she's taking off her cleats. "Glad you could make it, Andie!" she teases.

"How's the stomach?" Ivy asks.

"Sore," I reply honestly as I open my locker.

Caitlin sits down to untie her shoes. "These cleats are seriously uncomfortable," she complains as she pulls one off. "I don't know how you wear them for those long practices. And they don't go with anything —"

Suddenly, the door flies open and Maddie rushes in. "There you are! Oh my gosh! Cait! What happened, are you okay?" she asks in a flurry. "Are you sick? I mean. That was so weird! What happened to your piece? I kept waiting for you to —" Suddenly, she stops and stares at the two of us, both in soccer clothes and ponytails.

"Cait?" she asks, looking from Caitlin to me and back. "Andie?" she tries to correct herself, but clearly isn't sure who is who. She throws her arms up in the air, then folds them neatly across her chest and eyes us suspiciously. "Something's not right here," she says pointedly.

Caitlin, Tara, Ivy, and I all look at each other and burst out laughing. "You can say that again," I agree. Then everyone starts talking at once.

Maddie holds up her hands. "One at a time, please!" she begs. And we all laugh again. Then we quickly change into our regular clothes, and our regular selves, and follow Maddie outside while Caitlin explains it all.

CHAPTER NINETEEN
♪ CaitLin ♩

"And then we had to switch again," I tell Maddie. "Andie needed my identity so she could hang out with Scooter and not embarrass herself. . . ." I shoot my sister a look to let her know that I'm just kidding, but TarandIvy are giggling so hard that I'm pretty sure it's not me she's worried about.

"Sandchucker Scooter!" Tara squeals.

"Perpetual-Popsicle-Mustache Scooter!" Ivy adds with a snort.

"Yeah, but he's actually kind of cute now," I say with a little smile. "Don't tell me you haven't noticed. And have you seen the guy play soccer? Even I can tell that he is seriously good, and I don't go for the sporty type."

"Thank you, Caitlin," Andie says gratefully as we walk down the hall. Andie jogs ahead of us, then turns around so we are facing each other.

"Okay, so the gang's all here!" she quips. I can tell she's trying not to sound nervous about everyone knowing she likes Scooter, but her voice sounds a little funny. She made me nervous, but I am just relieved to have everything out in the open, and glad to have all my friends around me — it makes wallowing in my no-Jazz-Ensemble misery a little harder to do. But then, with a jolt, I realize that the gang is *not* all here. Someone is missing.

"Hey, wait!" I cry. "Olive is still auditioning!"

Andie slaps her head, and we all take off running to the multipurpose room. We slide in the double doors at the back of the darkened room just in time to see the end of Olive's audition. And even from the little bit we see I know that her Sandy is totally great. At the end of her last song she takes a little bow, walks off the stage, and saunters up to us. She tries not to smile but just can't help it. A second later she is grinning from ear to ear.

"I am so glad you made it," she whispers, walking right up to me.

"I'm Caitlin," I tell her a little nervously while I check to make sure that my hair is down.

She pauses for just a second, then squeezes my hand. "I know." She beams.

And at that moment I know that with a sister like Andie and friends like Maddie and Olive — and even TarandIvy — I can live without Jazz Ensemble . . . at least for one more year.

We sling our arms around one another in a long row and head out to the grass in the front of the school. But as soon as we're out there, Olive, who is in between me and Andie, wheels around in front of us, leaving one hand on one of each of our shoulders. "All right, you two, I may be the actor here, but you guys have been putting on your own little performance, and I think it's time for you to come clean."

TarandIvy and Maddie all giggle.

Andie hangs her head, and I start to explain all over again.

"We weren't trying to pull anything on *you*," I insist earnestly. "But we had to switch. I mean, I had to pass the fitness test so I could do Jazz Ensemble after school. And I was absolutely positive there was no way *I* could do it."

"And there was no way to tell all of you since we swore we wouldn't try to trick you after what happened last time," Andie adds. "Remember how mad you were?"

"It was only supposed to be a one-shot deal. Nobody finds out, nobody gets hurt," I say weakly.

"So what happened?" Olive asks, cocking an eyebrow.

"Well, then I sort of accidentally made Andie into a Mathlete, and Andie made me into a boy-crazy soccer girl —"

"Hey!" Andie objects.

"Boy crazy?" Olive's eyes widen.

"It's true!" TarandIvy chorus.

"And, well, it just kind of escalated from there," I finish, realizing how utterly ridiculous it all sounds.

Olive smiles and pulls us both into a giant hug. "All's well that ends well, right?" she says. "And now I have *both* of you back." She pushes back and holds us at arm's length. "But you have to promise you won't pull any more sister switches . . . without telling all of us first," she adds with a grin. "Deal?"

"Deal," Andie and I say together.

"We might be able to get away with being each other, but we are waaaaay better at being our-selves," Andie adds. I couldn't agree more.

"You can say that again." Tara giggles.

"No way did Andie pull off 'musician,'" Maddie giggles. "You should have seen, I mean heard, her. Actually, you should all be grateful you didn't have to!"

I force a smile. All may be well that ends well, but I'm still disappointed.

Olive turns to me, looking serious. "So you didn't even get to play the piece you've been practicing?" she asks.

Tarandlvy look a little guilty. "Um, I think she was supposed to be doing that when we were making her play soccer as Andie," Tara admits.

"Will you play it for us?" Olive asks.

"Oh yes!" Maddie says.

"Great idea!"

Everyone starts clamoring to hear me play, which makes me proud and embarrassed at the same time.

"I don't have my clarinet," I protest, a little lamely. Because the truth is, I really want to play. I've worked so hard preparing my piece for an audience. And I have a feeling that playing it for *this* audience might not make me sick. In fact, I think it might make me feel better.

Andie grins and pulls the black case out of my bag. "I do!" she chortles.

So I take the clarinet out of its case and get to my feet. I look at my sister's and my friends' faces, then close my eyes and begin. I play the piece all the way through, every note perfectly, by heart. Even the finish is exactly right.

"Whooo-hooo!" Olive cheers the loudest, but everyone is clapping and whistling.

I bow dramatically, then plop down on the grass. "Too bad nobody else will ever hear it."

"There's always next year," Andie tells me, looking like she feels totally responsible.

"I'm afraid I don't want to wait until next year," a voice says. I whirl around and see that Mr. Kolb is standing behind me. Maddie is standing beside him, beaming. How long have they been back there?

"Look for your name on the list tomorrow. It will be posted outside the band room in the morning. It's Andie, isn't it?"

"No, that's Caitlin," Maddie corrects him, making us all crack up again.

"Well, I'm not sure what happened at your audition, but anyone who plays like you just did should definitely be in the ensemble."

I jump to my feet, resisting the urge to throw my arms around the music teacher. "I'd love to

join," I tell him as I feel my heart soar. Jazz
Ensemble! I get to play in Jazz Ensemble! "Thank
you so much! And don't worry," I add as I point
to my identical twin, who's not so totally different from me after all. "People get us confused all
the time!"

check out

ACCIDENTALLY FABULOUS

BY LISA papademetriou

another

candy apple book . . .

just for you.

"You've only got ten minutes to get to the bus, and I'm not driving you," Mom warned.

My brother Kirk and I gobbled the rest of our breakfast and headed down the block to the edge of the park.

I sighed. Sure enough, all of the kids at the bus stop had gotten onto the Lamar bus. Now I was standing at the corner by myself, feeling a little conspicuous. I wished that I had a novel in my bag. But I'd just finished reading my book and forgot to add a new one.

I was debating whether or not to study the ingredients in my Mentos when a humongous bus pulled up in front of me. It wasn't a school bus, though. It was super-tall, and had dark tinted glass—like the buses tourists ride around in. I stepped back just as the doors opened and a perky woman in a hunter green polo shirt and khaki pants stepped out. She looked down at her clipboard, then up at me. "Amy Flowers?" she asked.

I was so surprised that I just nodded.

The woman flapped her fingers at me in a Get on the Bus gesture, and that was when I noticed that her polo shirt said Allington Academy in the upper left corner. It was written on the bus, too, in small, tasteful gold letters near the door. *Whoa—this is my* school *bus? Insanity.*

I climbed the stairs into the shiny, plush interior of the bus. It was cool inside—the air conditioning felt wonderful. It was still late August in Houston, and even though it wasn't even eight in the morning, it was hot.

"Orange or sparkling?" the woman with the ponytail asked as the doors hissed closed and the bus pulled away from the curb.

I thought about that for a moment, but I couldn't make any sense out of the question. "Sorry?"

The woman sighed, as if it was particularly torturous to have to deal with someone as dumb as me this early in the morning. She exaggerated her lip movements and spoke very slowly as she explained, "Do you want orange juice or sparkling water?" She pointed to a cooler nearby that was packed with drinks.

"Oh," I said. "Uh, how much does it cost?"

The woman shook her head, like I really was the slowest person on the planet. "They're free," she said, like—duh, of course, doesn't every school bus hand out free beverages on the way to class? "The newspapers are free, too," she added.

It seemed like only minutes had passed when the bus pulled up to Allington. I'd been there before, of course, for a tour of the campus. But now, the masses of perfectly groomed students spilled in through the iron front gates and a line of luxury cars waited to pull up to the entrance.

Looking up at the large building, my heart gave a little flutter. *This is it,* I thought. *My first day at Allington Academy.*